THE PULL OF IT

Wendy J. Fox

Wendy J Fox

Underground Voices
Los Angeles, California
2016

Published by Underground Voices
www.undergroundvoices.com
Editor contact: Cetywa Powell
ISBN: 978-0990433170
Printed in the United States of America.

To Joel, on this journey.

CONTENTS

Parts of this manuscript have appeared in similar or different form in *The Coe Review, Apple Valley Review, Quiddity International Journal, The Puritan, Washington Square, Gemini Magazine, Midway Journal,* and *P·M·S | poemmemoirstory.*

THE PULL OF IT

CHAPTER ONE

The New Year's after I lost my job in the registrar's office at the university, my husband, Julian, and I got a sitter for our seven-year-old daughter, even though I always worried about holiday babysitters: What kind of teenager doesn't have anywhere to be on New Year's, and do I want to leave my kid with them? Julian, ever practical, told me to stop wondering so much about other people's lives. Truthfully, this did nothing for me: What kind of person doesn't wonder about other people's lives, and do I want to be married to him? But I said, "You're probably right."

I was thirty-five years old and had already been unemployed since the summer, and it was much scarier than I had thought it would be when layoffs were being discussed. All we'd hear in the Seattle news was that the dot-com bubble was bursting, bursting—pop!—but I hadn't thought how it would impact the private institution I worked for. Sure enough though, parents started pulling their students out and opting for lower state tuition.

When I packed up my office, I thought of how people sometimes described the Internet as *the web*, and I thought of myself unwittingly caught in it, like when I'd come out of the basement with a face full of spider silk. Even if it had not been spun for me, there it was, tangled around my eyelashes.

For the party that New Year's, we got dressed up in the way that we did then—in what I categorized as a *married* way, but it was really just our particular married way. Julian wore clean khakis and a pressed shirt; I made an effort by putting on a bra that wasn't ripped at the seams and a reasonable top over it with a skirt and a pair of beat up, low heels, plus I used mascara. And then we spent the evening at an averagely boring party, where I stared into what seemed like an always empty glass of gin and tonic, angrily thinking, *Who's being stingy with the goddamned limes?*

Julian was mingling and some of the other ladies were waxing on about how nice it was to have an evening without their children, while I wondered about our daughter and figured she was just as bored as I was, with the no-social-life babysitter. I wished we were curled on the sofa together, with me braiding her hair, or painting each other's nails—we would ignore Julian when he complained about the stink of the polish, when he talked about the chemicals—while doing our own silly countdown as the pre-recorded Times Square ball dropped. She loved the sparkle of it, I knew.

Without my husband directly in tow, I tried to mingle too, but I didn't like these types of parties where everyone was so deeply coupled that as the night wore on, the men separated into one room to play pool, if someone had a table, or into the garage to smoke cigars or pot, and the women kicked off their shoes and gathered in the living room to complain about their feet and their husbands, but I followed them anyway and found a seat on an armchair. This was when my drink started to feel even emptier, and the crusty, non-abundant limes even drier. While the men separated from the women, like curd from whey, I sat on the side

4

and let the host's dog lie down on the floor and drool across the tips of my toes that peeked out from the worn leather of my pumps. It didn't bother me and the dog seemed happy, and I thought if I could just stay still for a few minutes I would feel better. That the room would slow. That I would stop obsessing over what Anastasia, our daughter, was or was not doing.

There was a lull in the chatter, and someone finally said something about the dog, how he was gnawing around at my feet. I tried to wave her off, but she wouldn't listen, insisting my shoes were being ruined. *They were already ruined, honey,* I wanted to say, but I didn't. I got up from my chair and took the dog by the collar. I figured she must have a leash somewhere, but I didn't look for it. I refreshed my cocktail, found my coat, and when I was done I asked the dog to come with me by patting my skirt, crumpled and hairy, and she followed. Outside, it was cold, but not impossible. It was hardly ever very cold in Seattle, only damp, though sometimes the damp made me feel like someone had replaced my bone marrow with soggy lichens and soft moss.

I wished for Julian to join the dog and me and say it was time to go home. I wished to bring the friendly mutt in tow and save her for Anastasia, who would wake in the morning, groggy and incredulous and thrilled. Naming would commence: Buttons, Sugarcane, Rochelle, Fur Face.

It was quiet outside, in a suburban neighborhood. I could hear some hooting from the open window in the basement where the men had gathered, and could see the women's faces past the open drapes in the living room. It didn't look like they missed me. I leaned against a stone wall in the host's garden. There was some kind of slick fungus that I knew would leave a streak of green down my backside, but I didn't care. There was a low fog, but it wasn't actually raining, and that was a nice change for winter.

I was just outside the front door for what seemed like a long time. My drink was empty, but the ice was melting slowly. I started to hear the click of the latch on the front door opening and closing. People were leaving. The women had vacated the living room and the basement seemed empty. I watched for Julian to come through the door, and when he finally did, I stepped around a bush that had been shielding me and joined him.

"There you are," he said. "I looked everywhere."

"I was here the whole time," I said.

"Put that glass back in the kitchen. Don't steal their crystal."

I ran my finger around the rim to check, and the glass gave a low pitch, a little flat sounding from my other hand's grip, dampening the vibration.

"Laura," my husband said. "Please."

I went to the kitchen. I washed the glass, fingerprinted like a bad crime scene. The host told me to leave it, but I kept washing, slowly, so I would not break anything. The warm water felt good on my fingertips, and the detergent smelled of citrus and mint. I rinsed the glass for a long time before I placed it on the drain board.

When we left, we did not take the dog, and we did not take any leftovers.

Julian was angry, I could tell. One of my jobs in our married life was to not act weird at parties, especially parties hosted by people he worked with or hoped to work with. Sometimes I couldn't help it. I did things like let the dog drool on my shoes. Once at a political fundraiser, I had said, *Oh, I'm not even registered to vote,* even though I loved voting, especially for judges and school board members. Frequently, I slipped outside to sneak cigarettes.

I had forgotten to ask Julian if he was okay to drive, but he seemed fine. We were in a smooth space after the first rush of people leaving parties and before the bars let out. The radio was playing the BBC America broadcast. Outside, the streets looked cool, matte from several days of no rain.

I remembered when we had our own New Year's parties, when we were new and lived in a series of small apartments, and prayed the neighbors wouldn't complain, and the plumbing wouldn't be tested too hard. We always kept a tower of keg cups stashed under the sink or in some high cabinet, if we had it, because it didn't take much time to run out of our own chipped stoneware and dinged glasses. More than once I had tipped bargain champagne from red plastic, heard the *thunk* when toasting against our one proper flute, seen the crimson debris scattered around whichever place we were living in the next morning, me with a hangover scrubbing at the spills on the floorboards, and Julian washing the dishes that hadn't been broken.

One year, we had three guests who couldn't organize a taxi because they were too high, and the waits were so long at 2 in the morning when the clubs had closed and the house gatherings had fizzled out. In the meantime they'd fallen asleep on our floor. I didn't want them to stay, but after the first one started to snore, there was no stopping it, so I'd tossed a few blankets and a pillow without a case on top of their jumble of limbs, flicked off the living room light, and shrugged.

In our tiny bedroom, just a few feet away, Julian said I should feel happy they felt so comfortable in our home. I said at least they were passed out and wouldn't be having noisy sex. I remembered we giggled, doing what we thought sounded like their voices under our own blanket. We weren't even sure who had brought them; they weren't our friends, we were just keeping them—until the sun began to break the dark.

Just as we finally dozed off, the man of our overnight guests was up in our kitchen, brewing coffee and flipping eggs in a skillet. He'd made biscuits, from scratch, and after he'd managed to rouse everyone with his cooking, banging a cast iron pan against the stove and singing old folk songs in a low but urgent voice, the five of us sat cross-legged on the floor in a pretty circle with mismatched plates, and not everyone with a napkin, because we were out of nearly everything, including towels and toilet paper.

Of the women, one's hair had remained remarkably intact and the other's was a stunning disarray of bobby pins, haphazard bangs, and feathers. The man was shaved bald, and he asked us if we minded if he said grace, and everyone murmured that it would be just fine.

Bless this home and these people, who have let us rest on their accommodating if hard floor. The memory of their wine eases the hurt in our hips, yet brings a new hurt to our heads. On this morning, the first morning of a glorious new year, we pray that all souls feel the bounty of hospitality, which we suggest might include some aspirin. We pray for friendship among strangers, and we pray for happy endings. We travel in a world of ripped petticoats and worn-out boots, but praise the moments we can forget this with dancing, amen.

Then we smeared butter and yolk across our warm bread: a gift, culled from a bag of aging flour and expired baking soda.

I rummaged in the bathroom until I found some ibuprofen, and handed out the little blue lozenges like a coveted drug, placing each one on the tip of their outstretched tongues.

When the meal was done and the plates were collected, the man and his ladies thanked us for our generosity and he excused himself for digging in our cupboards. Our pleasure, we exclaimed, already working at the cleanup, dipping our hands into a tub of suds. We never saw them again.

I supposed our life was different now.

A shepherd might not know who her foundling will turn out to be, but loves him anyhow.

The long line of marriage is like that.

I supposed he could have left me there instead of looking, but my husband led me stumbling and chilled to our car, and then he took us home.

•

Before I met Julian, I lived with my lover, a country boy, who could have been one of my brothers. We liked to think we weren't really hilljacks (this was my word for it) anymore, since we'd gone off to college in Seattle and stayed in the city. Washington State is divided by the Cascades, and on the other side of those tall, irregular volcanoes was a different world from what we had known, growing up rural in the high desert, surrounded by orchards and wheat. It took us some time to get used to all the water. We'd been raised to speak of rain the way some folk speak of the dead: with longing, without hope for return. The water from the sound flanked us, the water from the sky kept us cold. Sometimes I'd make coffee in the mornings and there would be a bloom of fungi on the kitchen windowsill, tiny stems and caps. I'd scrub the casement, chips of wood coming off on my rag. I always washed my hands carefully after. The only experience we had of mushrooms growing up was hunting for morels after a wildfire would cut through the forest behind our childhood homes.

But the thing about country people is they can be moved to a new geography, be thrust into the routines that seem normal for the rest of the world, but they still have the dirt in them. They still feel the kickback of a rifle on their shoulder, they still expect trouble.

More than once, in those hot summers, I'd push aside a curtain of fireweed—a tall, stalky plant with magenta petals that grew taller than if one of us stood on the other's shoulders, and whose roots loved the hot, tender soil of a recent fire—and find him, waiting just off the trail for me.

We were neighbors, which meant a mile or so between our homes.

My lover, my childhood friend—the one I did not marry, that I could not—was a year younger than me, so I'd left our small hometown before him. We'd grown apart some too, so I was not in regular touch with him. At first, we'd moved fairly anonymously through our shared university campus. I had heard he was coming to the same school as me, because it was news. Not many of us left our little hamlet, but I hadn't thought to call his mother and get his address or a phone number. I figured, like me, he probably didn't have a phone. Yet, through a drizzle one day I saw him in the commons, and I thought, *I know you.* I'd grown up with this boy. He'd pissed in streams with my brothers, our parents were friends, and we'd spent days together as children plotting against the tyranny of adults. And for the next several months, I spotted him almost every day, but I ignored him because he was proof of the place I'd left. I was working hard to build a different kind of life.

One day, in a coffee shop off campus, just as my graduation neared, he stopped me. He said he only wanted to say hello. He said, *It has been hard for me here. I thought maybe we could talk.*

Sometimes when someone reaches for you, you reach back.

•

I have a memory of me young, my brothers and me, when we were just a girl and some boys in eastern Washington, all piled onto my parent's brown sofa. It was summer and I was in a typical summer dress, frayed hem, the fabric itself a non-color from being washed and worn and worn more than it was washed.

I was just on the cusp of adolescence, and maybe I hadn't really learned yet what people can do to other people, though even at a young age, country children know something of the ugliness of adults.

Country children are not kind. They live close to animals and the dirt, turning the idyllic forests and fields into battlegrounds. They learn to handle weapons, to slaughter fowl and four-leggeds. They are accustomed to hides and gasoline, and being out in all kinds of weather. And they also learn to protect themselves, because they have eaten their pet piglets, watched their seedlings die, chopped the heads off of snakes with the barn shovels, and they have not learned to believe that they are any different, any less immune to brutality. They know that the same heart that pushes blood through their veins will just as happily push it out of an exit wound.

This, though, was not one of those violent times. My brothers, Michael at the foot of the couch and Richard, the youngest, on the cushions by me, had been perfectly quiet for several minutes, and so had I.

Often I came back to us like this, our six bare dirty feet and unwashed hands, our shiny eyes, our lips pressed closed. It was rare that our bodies were so close, rare that we as a group resembled anything like still. Usually we were covered in mud and tumbling into or out of something.

We were facing the wall. Our parents had a little television, but it wasn't on, and we didn't notice. It was not quite stinking hot yet, but it would be soon, and we seemed to have promptly forgotten what we came for.

I remember I felt like inertia was the thing I was made of, instead of my usual: all raging, tender guts.

I wanted to fold into Michael; he was only two years younger than me, but I already felt us pulling apart, and I wanted to haul Richard into my lap, even though at six he was too old for it. Both of them, as children, were as blond as wheat; we all sunburned.

And then, more than closeness, I wanted deep promises from them. I wanted to hear Richard, who was as menacing as soap, say something fierce or wicked; I wanted Mikey to join him, and I wanted them to swear their allegiances to each other and then, finally to me. I thought *They are my brothers and I love them*, and I wanted proof.

It passed though. The screen door slammed in the wind or maybe one of them burped and we all remembered there were popsicles—which to us were generally just ice with a toothpick rammed into the cube, or if we were lucky, frozen orange juice from a can—or that we had a captured grasshopper waiting in a glass jar to have her legs ripped off, or that we were in a fight, and we got up and went back to our day.

Years later, I was the first generation college student visiting home after a successful year at university, and Mikey had taken the GED to get out of high school a year early. He was studying for his welding certificate at a technical college, and I saw suddenly how his hair had gone brown, how his face became rough in the afternoon, how his hands, already, had the thick broken skin of a man who works with them. Richard was still small to me; he had become slim and inward, and like his brother, a brunette. He mostly stayed in his room and listened to his albums. For months.

I didn't know what had happened to them, my boys. It was more than growing up. It was absence. I realized I didn't have anything to say to them, that I had rarely thought of them in the past year, that I had come to my parent's home mostly out of a habit I was trying to break.

This is what distance does.

A decade and a half later—less time than we'd spent together—we three lived in three places so different that we didn't experience the same seasons, and when we looked at the sky, our horizons would not be recognizable to one of the others.

•

Daniel, the boy from my hometown, courted me in a way that seemed appropriate and familiar. A friend of his parents' had given him a busted-up pickup and we drove out to the gray northern Pacific beaches and said nothing for a long time while collecting broken sand dollars. We rode the ferries out to the islands, had a coffee, and came back. Once we took the train to Portland. We'd grown up always wanting to disappear from where we were, and it was hard to shake the habits of leaving.

He was thin and soft, and like a bridge between one world and the next.

By the time we moved in to a house on Fauntleroy together, I thought I was a tasseographer of his body.

I watched him.

He came home one day with a bruise on his upper thigh, and the more it came out, the more it looked like the shape of a mouth instead of a run-in with the corner of a table like he'd said. I wondered who had bit him so hard he couldn't tell me; I wondered who had tried to take him whole in her mouth. I knew the other marks of his body—the crescent scar above his left eye (like the similar one above my right), the raspberry on his shoulder from being hit very, very hard by a baseball decades ago (the summer he was fourteen), and one long permanent scratch down his index finger (his otherwise perfect hands).

We were both graduated by then, but I was having problems at my job. I worked as the office manager at a construction company. I had also discovered psychiatry. Sometimes I'd take twice my usual Zoloft before I went to work just so I could be serotonin -stoned because it gave the morning a thick, underwater feeling that I liked. My employer, a small contractor, was close to where we lived. I did permitting and paperwork, mostly, which I was very good at, when I tried.

The drugs, if I took extra, would wrench my gut, and occasionally—before I got a tolerance going—I'd throw up and my boss would let me go home. If I'd driven Daniel's truck, it took me a whole three minutes to get back to our house; if I'd walked, maybe more like fifteen.

I really did do good work when I paid attention, but considering how much time I'd taken to spending in the bathroom, my boss was unhappy with me, and while I knew it, I couldn't do anything about it because of the trouble that had started with Daniel.

By the time all this was happening, we found out I was pregnant, and our shared childhood of me— because I was the older one—forcing him to play house looked like it might come true. I should say when *he* found out I was pregnant, because I knew from day one. I've heard it is like that sometimes. He was already asking me questions because he'd bring me a beer and I couldn't finish it. Just physically couldn't.

When I bought the box of tests, there were two inside, individually wrapped. The first was a dud. No response. I had to wait another hour before I could pee again and the feeling was pretty clear—I was being stalled. I didn't need to wait and see the **X** poking through the plastic window on the white plastic stick, but it worked all right for me as a confirmation, and a way to tell him. I dropped the test on the kitchen table, and he said I had to stop taking the Zoloft, but I didn't.

And, I didn't ask Daniel about the bruise, though I wanted to. I wanted to shake the words out of him and have them spit into my hand like a set of milk teeth. One night, when it had turned green before it faded out, I made a batch of cornbread and brought it to him with butter while he read in the living room. He wanted to know why I'd baked it, but I couldn't say why, except that I had a craving. So maybe he got his bruise like that—a little impulse made real. We sat on the sofa and had our respective squares and he said *this is really good* and I said *thanks* and that was all; we ate in the half-dark, our teeth cutting all the way through.

It was a long way for us to land in Seattle, together, where the air was damp like a body. There were mushrooms growing around the window casements of our house, but we didn't mind. Sometimes we'd stand out in the perpetual rain, wet up to the shins in our tall, never-mowed grass, and tip our heads back to the sky. Nothing could burn us in that town, and for the two of us, who held the same dark scars of perpetual summer forest fires where we'd grown up, on the tinder-dry side of the state, this was a blessing. We were soaked and we stayed soaked.

When I think about it now, though, I think maybe he wasn't so grateful for all that water we were surrounded by, water from west, water from the ground, water from the sky.

After the cornbread day, everything in the house started dying. My houseplants drooped. Fruit spoiled. The yard smelled like yeast. Especially if I was alone, I'd find smells lurking all over. I remembered once in my

17

family home, a winter when the owls had gotten bold and carried off all of our cats, and finally, the mice began to take over.

My father, if he found one, would catch it in a jar and throw it into the woodstove. He was not unkind to animals as a general rule but had a deep vendetta towards rodents and starlings. Finally, we had to put out poison, which worked much better than Dad's method. Our mice filled their guts and then slunk off into the walls to die. The smell of fur and bellies being eaten from the inside out hung inside for a good week.

With Daniel and me—or maybe just me—it was just a rotten, unplaceable stink. Maybe it was the pregnancy but I had clods of hair coming out and plugging the drain. There was a black spot on the gum above my right incisor.

I guess I was as sick as those mice then. Daniel said I had taken to talking in my sleep; I did not know if it was true, but I did know that my dreams were restless and for the first time in many years, I could not remember them. I knew that I would wake and be startled or disoriented and he would say, *I'm here*, and though I pushed my body into his, I wasn't always so sure he was what I needed.

I had a desperate feeling about him—that I wanted him and wanted him gone at the same time. That is a feeling something like fear. It is a feeling that a moth must feel, driven to chew her way out of the cocoon, terrified at what she might find.

What I mean is I was open to the possibility of disaster, to the trouble we were so used to.

I don't like to admit how suspicious I was. I was suspicious of everything, not only of Daniel, though I was preoccupied with the bruise. It was real, by all definitions: I could see it, I could feel it raised from his skin; I knew it would taste bitter in my mouth.

I liked to say that I had known him since he was born. Probably this is true. Probably when I was screaming at eleven months old and he was screaming, even newer to the world, I knew him. Our mothers, if not fast friends, were neighbors. There was only a mile or two separating our families. I remembered once, in deep summer, walking to Daniel's to play and hearing the terrifying *tsktsktsktsk* of rattlesnakes. I didn't know whether to keep going or to go home, so I kept going. It seemed shorter. I never saw a snake, and a day later, cicadas bloomed across the fields and destroyed the alfalfa and the gardens, and I felt silly for being so terrified—the cicadas were scary in their own right, but not like a rattler.

One night, in the Fauntleroy house Daniel kicked open one of the low cabinet doors in the kitchen and hiked his leg up to rest his foot on the top near the hinge, and I saw our history in him. He'd let his hair go wild. I said he looked like Walt Whitman. He played songs on his guitar, and then after, counted out the timing to help me understand how he'd made them.

Another thing that was a problem was that in the evening I would start crying. I said I couldn't stop crying, but I didn't *want* to stop. When I cried, he'd hold onto me like he craved every slope of my skin, not like I was just the default body around the house.

Then the grass went dormant and the roses dried up. Not that we'd ever taken care of the roses. And, I had always loved how the morning glories snaked through our yard, a takeover done all in white, but our landlord came and hacked at what was left of the under-tended beds. Mostly, after the roses keeled over and the blooming weeds were ripped out, all she had left to do was pull mint that had gone infestive and poke at some stubby rhododendrons.

Still, I was angry at the pile of vines composting over by the recycling. We lived there, and we paid for it, and it seemed like if I wanted the yard to be more of a thicket I could have it that way. Daniel said that was not really the way it worked.

I guess I didn't have a lot of sympathy for him, sometimes.

Did he think I thought his bruise was only a smear of charcoal? We didn't use wood-burning stoves anymore, like we had as children, when our evening chores would include hauling in wood in winter and stacking wood in summer.

I thought he was leaving me.

I *knew* he was leaving me and I was enraged.

The morning glories were nothing.

What did we do then? We'd share some poems, swap a song or two, and then hunker down on the couch with our cornbread. Chewing.

All of which is to say, I blamed the pregnancy and I blamed our shared memories, but neither of us were absolved. There is not enough water in this world for our ablutions. I read once that the Koran says if there's no water around it's okay to use dirt or sand as long as the body parts get done in the right order. The point is that people try. So, okay. Maybe we weren't trying. I felt pretty tried out, actually.

I suppose he and I had grown up doing enough farming that we should have expected the weather would turn on us. The rain helped him find the mouth that bit the bruise into his leg; the rain licked me between my thighs and found my belly. The rain made my head mushy.

In the Fauntleroy house, it was like a thousand years had passed. Maybe we were fated. I think sometimes I felt more like his sister than his lover. When we met again, we were reluctant to tell our families or anyone we knew from home. But why else would he have found me, if not to take our lives back from the ash of that place?

But then again, I was pregnant and he was bitten. Neither one of us were exactly at our best. Also, we were having too many Very Long Talks. Mostly he was distressed and scared about what was happening in my body. Mostly I was distressed and scared about what I could see on his.

Then one day, I put on the kettle to make tea and forgot about it. I'd taken the whistler out of the spout because I didn't like the screech. Yes, it was caffeinated, and I wasn't supposed to be having caffeine, but the tea soothed me, and I saved the bags for my eyes, which were swollen a lot. It was awhile before we smelled it, the scorch of metal on metal. We both went running for the kitchen. When I lifted the kettle off the burner, he said *Careful,* and he said it so softly I nearly dropped the pot—it was startling to hear his whisper.

Then I didn't know what to think, because it seemed like a little accident, like forgetting the tea water caused so much to turn. Because after that, I wasn't actually pregnant anymore. There wasn't a lot of blood or anything like that, but I think whoever was in there decided to get us on the next round. I felt like one of those small, drafty houses from our childhood after that. I did feel like I was back in the moondust landscape we used to live in. I did smell sage constantly, though it certainly didn't grow close to the Fauntleroy house. I did realize that combustion isn't as simple as I'd thought—he and I might have landed in a wet clime, but there was still all kinds of smolder. Think of how a stack of wet rags or pile of compost might ignite: slowly, and without the drama of a match, of gasoline, of the sky's electricity. It's almost worse.

So there we were. Fire makes some soft things, like wood, hard; or the heat causes little fissures to explode. I guess it works that way on insides, because we split then. I hadn't wanted to think that he was just hanging around because he'd accidentally knocked me up, but there I had it.

How terrified I was, how sad. When we packed up our things it was like there was nothing left of the time we'd spent in the house. I was scared to touch him, as much as I wanted to feel his skin. I asked him if he was going off to his lover, the one who had bruised him. He was hauling something and he said, *Stop looking at me like that, don't look at me,* so I did. I stopped.

I moved into a house with some friends from college, and I spent a lot of time on the porch, in the rain after work, and I would think, *This is what it's like to be stuck.* I would think, *This is exactly what I was trying to avoid.* I would miss Daniel. Sometimes I would make a batch of cornbread and throw it out. I would sit out on the porch so I wouldn't have to smell it. My roommates left me alone.

From my seat outside, I would watch the cars go by, the Nissans and Fords and Volkswagens. I was always good at recognizing the make or model of a car, but their years eluded me. Then, on a larger scale, I could not have said what part of time I fit into.

What I was experiencing was a lack of concentration.

What I was experiencing was not an experience at all, but a state.

What I was experiencing was the way the things, which aren't really things at all, like light, attach to the body and make it glow. I would close my eyes and see someone grinding grain on a grist wheel, or one dirty-faced boy snapping his stick at a herd of calves, all outlined like an after-image of staring at the sun.

And I would see Daniel, from the time we were children, from the time when my brothers and I still knew each other, from the time when we believed that leaving the farmlands would erase that time of our life. I heard that he had moved back home, and though I wanted to follow him there, I resisted it. I felt a little tougher, a little more cacti, a little less moss. But Daniel's skin—I could see his skin clearly, as impeccably smooth as water. And, like water, maybe there would be movement underneath, or maybe a group of thrashing kids would wreck the plane with a cascade of rocks. I started to believe I was wrong about the bruise, because no matter what happened, no matter how I could see him ripple to the touch or his surface scar briefly, he would go back to perfect every time.

What bound us was not our time on Fauntleroy, but the year of the fire, when we were so young, when it had not rained for months. Maybe it was a decade with no rain; it felt like no one knew. I remembered the sizzle of everything, the way my hair became dried and broken at the ends, and I was all static and dust. My parents' well was failing. Our yard was long gone, and the lilac bush slumped against the side of the house, blooms dropped and drying around the base. The strawberry beds and the raspberries were paper. We had a plot of wilty potatoes, a cherry tree, and brittle greens, though nearby our southern neighbor's heat-loving wheat fields glowed as gold as a pharaoh's polished tomb. The fields were on a plateau, where the land was mostly flat and open, but there were a few pines poking out through the yellow stalks or fallow dirt; shade and topsoil were precious, and the farmer had not wanted to cut the trees or destroy the root systems that held the ground in place when the wind blew, even if it meant extra turns on the combine.

Our year of water would not make Daniel nor I forget the night the fire started—thunder all afternoon and then finally, lightning—I hadn't seen him and didn't know where he had been that day because I'd been absorbed in a stack of old, over-thumbed magazines my mother had brought home. It was hot. If I stayed perfectly still, I was almost comfortable, but the minute I moved, the heat would swirl around me like when I ran bathwater with too much red and not enough blue.

I remembered how clearly I wanted night to come and along with it the promise of at least a minute of cool; but instead, the sky opened, electric.

My mother let me stay up past midnight, so we could watch the hillside blaze. Even from miles off I heard the sound of the trees exploding, a hundred years of pine gone. I don't know how I felt besides awe for the ignition, or if I had a sense of the way flame moved.

A day or two later, after little success, as our fathers scratched at the dirt with their axes, trying to loosen enough earth to suffocate the flames, the families on our rural mountainside tried to control-burn their own land and barns before the lightning fire got there— an attempt to leave no fuel so they could at least save the houses. The roads closed. The gardens were singed. Our mothers cooked whatever they could find to feed their lovers and husbands, grown and half-grown sons, including a pig they took down with little more than a kitchen knife. Any one of them would have known how to handle a small rifle, but even circled by fire, they killed her the clean way—bled her into a trough before the gutting.

Perhaps my mother did this. She was good with a blade. In my short lifetime I couldn't count the number of chickens I'd seen her behead—picking them up by their legs, flinging them onto a round of wood, and lopping them off at the neck. They really will run for a bit, but it's only a second or two.

They decided then to evacuate the children and send them to live for a few days in the nondenominational church in town. In the heat, we watched a helicopter landing among the wheat, and Daniel was there with me perched in the back of a silver van with heart-shaped windows. Where were my brothers, his sister? I didn't know. But I sat next to him in our getaway vehicle, his sunflower hair and eggplant eyes, and I prayed nothing would separate us, ever. Another helicopter landed—we were children who played war and who would chop the heads off snakes with a shovel or a sharp rock, but we had never seen anything like these *choppers*, as we so expertly called them—dropping enough buckets of red fire retardant to make a little portal along the roads, and that's when we went speeding through in the silver van on the way to the church, and we watched another huge machine touch down among the charred alfalfa and the ruined crop.

We hadn't known we were in danger, until we left it.

My parents kept their home, their barn, their outbuildings. Their upper tract burned, but, ultimately, we were out little. Even our well came back and came back clean. I had a pony—not a fancy ribbon-in-his-hair pony, but a work pony with lower GI distress, who farted constantly when he walked, and he got a stick in his eye, but one of my father's friends extracted it.

Daniel, though, lost nearly everything. All that was left, by the rock outcropping where his parents had built, was a blackened concrete foundation slab where the house had been. The chicken coop stood, though even the chickens, set free in the evacuation, were ash. It didn't take long for his parents to move down into town, our first separation.

I hadn't known there would be a harder one.

•

Maybe comparatively, Julian and I hadn't been married that long, but it felt like a long time. We'd been in our late twenties, and it had happened quickly. When I met Julian, I was still healing from Daniel and I didn't want to see anyone in any kind of a real way. I was thinking that I needed to refocus, and I'd been applying for new jobs and considering moving to another part of town. My roommates were some girls I knew from school, but it was clear that any friendship we shared had dissolved during the time I'd spent with Daniel. Mostly we said hello, I left my rent in cash and didn't argue about the utility bill, even though I was not the one staying up late with the lights blazing (I sat in the dark), and I was not the one taking long showers and shaving my legs (I didn't care, and washed my hair only infrequently). Finally, I moved out into a studio apartment that had a view of the adjoining building and had spotted mold on the ceiling in the bathroom, but was only a few blocks from public access to Lake Union.

I went to work, I tried to pay attention, but I couldn't stop thinking about him, and our shared childhood, the way it had tangled us together, and how quickly we'd been able to unravel it.

Sometimes, when angry all over again at Daniel, and tired of my roommates, I'd go to a show and pick out someone I thought I might be able to fuck, and usually I was right about it. It was easy to organize:

1. Take a long look at a candidate. Make sure he knows you are staring at him and not the crowd by holding eye contact.
2. Separate yourself from any part of a group you may be in by approaching the bar for another cocktail or strategically timing a visit to the restroom.
3. When he is near, turn to him as if you have been waiting, FOREVER.
4. Introduce yourself.
5. Remember that the trick is not pretending not to care if he's interested, it's actually not caring.
6. Ask him questions, and be flexible with his existing plans.
7. Smile!

That's how I met Julian. Once, one of these men was him, when the band was very loud, the room very dark. I only saw him because we were standing close to one another and were almost exactly the same height. Sometimes when a band played a slow, moody song, the earnest dancing would halt, and I, like every other person not coupled, would tip my head and rock to myself, as if in prayer.

Julian and I were both alone, weaving in and out of the sway of bodies, while we juggled our beers, navigating like we were underwater through a slow, murky crush. It was summer and I was wearing shorts, and I felt the wisps of the other women's skirts at my legs, sea anemone billowing for prey; but these, instead of shrinking at first touch, swirled around the smooth skin of my shins and ankles.

I scooted through a few more people—a man with dreadlocks that touched his waist, a woman whose shoes were glossy and pointed, ready for some sexy combat—yet stood perfectly still; at the same time he was coming towards me, and in a few seconds we were up against one another, saying, *Hello*, saying, *I like this band*, saying, *What's your name?* Saying anything that could be heard over the long wail of guitar. There was just a second in between the finish of one song and the start of the next that I could hear my own breath, and this man turned his face and looked at me and laced his fingers through mine, and even though in that moment, I wished he was Daniel, I squeezed his hand hard and didn't look away.

Maybe he was another one who was a little bit different, just like Daniel. I thought this in the morning, when he was leaving, when the light from my window caught his hair and it reminded me of yellow, on a spectrum of marigold blooms to straw to fresh butter. We hadn't had sex, only kissed heavily and then fallen asleep. I remembered how Daniel used to turn to me, and I'd see just the shadow of his face, and then there was this man, Julian, looking me straight on.

I remembered that I thought I'd said, *Don't go*, but I'd actually said it aloud.

"Hey," he said, "It's just that I promised brunch with my friend, and I have to get a cab to my car. I can come back if you'll be here."

"I live here," I said.

"Right," he said, and looked around the small room that was my apartment, jammed with clothes and books and compact discs of bands I liked loose from their cases. "How about I pick you up around four," he said. "We can go over to my place."

Then, when we were new, Julian did come back, on the dot, to gather me up in an old car with ripped seats and a howling engine. I liked him all over again because he was not ashamed of his shabby coach, didn't say anything about it, even; and despite its sounds, he drove it expertly, easing into each gear. I liked this about him, because I was from the country; I was used to busted-down trucks and other vehicles, the grind of gears and the smell of gasoline.

The seats smelled of tobacco and the windshield was cracked on the passenger side. Even though the Seattle summer was not especially hot, the vinyl stuck to my thighs and I could also feel the rumble of the failing exhaust vibrating the seat.

We were both a few years out of college by then. It had been a year and half since Daniel and I had split our things and left Fauntleroy. When I counted it on my fingers, it seemed like so many months, and it also seemed like nothing against how many years I'd known him. I'd called his parents a few times, asking after him, and all they ever said was that he knew where to find me if he wanted to, and they hung up. Sometimes I'd call back, later in the night, thinking they'd be asleep and I might catch him waiting for someone else. I didn't even know that he lived there, it was just the only place I could imagine him being other than with me. I'd be thinking about the little house we shared, I'd be thinking about how we almost became parents together, and how no one knew about it but us. No one ever picked up, though, and I'd listen to the line ring and ring, until the machine clicked on and started in on the same message I'd heard a hundred times before.

Julian helped me forget.

That day we went to his apartment, only a few steps larger than mine. He had a futon mattress on the bare floor, a cubby for dishes, a bathroom with drizzly water that knocked through the pipes like a disaster was coming.

I learned he had a marginally paying job for an environmental law firm as a policy researcher.

I told him about how one of the project managers at my work had called me a *libertine*, and I had rolled my eyes at him because I thought he was stupid and old, but when I was back at my desk, I had to look it up—*Libertine: a person who is unrestrained by convention or morality*—and I couldn't imagine where he'd ever come up with this word or where he might have heard it before, but I also didn't want to ask him.

"He's got the hots for you probably," Julian said.

"He's beyond married," I said. "He's got a whole unhappy family." We laughed at this.

In Julian's apartment, sometimes, even though it was warm, the radiator would steam to life, and we'd push the one window that looked onto the adjacent building just a little bit higher.

It was like opening an eye.

•

Before I lost my job, when students would tell me they were getting ready to walk down the aisle, I thought there was no way they could know what they were doing. Some of them were really only a few years younger than I had been. There was no way I'd known what I was doing, either.

We'd been lucky though. Julian and I had managed to stay kind to each other through some tricky parts, like growing up, like having a baby. We didn't fight, or at least not much. He had that beautiful, curly golden hair that our daughter had inherited. He brought me coffee in bed in the morning, after I'd stayed up too late reading or had too much wine, and held the mug to my nose instead of shaking me awake. When I lost my job, he shrugged and said that we'd figure it out. The day of my notice, I came home crying after having already cried the whole way home, tears smearing my view of the commute, making me, an otherwise cautious driver, dangerous on the road. I hadn't loved the job, but it paid well, and I had liked my colleagues enough that some had become real friends. Also, I knew there would be a deep discount from the school for our daughter, if I could just hang until she was college-aged. We could afford it either way, but I had wanted to give this to her, an open door. *Tuition's almost free—study painting! Dance! Sculpture! Do a year abroad! Screw accounting!*

My parents would have handed me this same kind of freedom if they could. I didn't doubt that. I didn't have so much luxury to find myself. My goal had been to become employable outside of the cherry sheds and the lumberyards.

Julian and I, during our young years when we'd scrabbled, had dreamed of a time when we could take a little vacation or shop at the organic markets instead of the grocery outlet, and while we'd gotten there, through sheer force of will, mostly, neither one of us had forgotten how it was to feel lucky to eek out an education through scholarships.

We were both grateful—and proud—but neither of us expected our daughter to take this route. We wanted to give it to her. We wanted her not to worry. We wanted her to have the luxury of growing up to believe she could do anything. It was true, that at the private school, sometimes I flinched at the students and what I thought was their overdeveloped sense of entitlement, but it was also true I wanted this for my girl, wanted to see her walk in confidently to an adult's office and *demand* that she be heard. Sometimes Anastasia would come home with a story of unfairness, telling us about some of the average childhood injustices: mean kids, indifferent teachers, bad lunches. She was so indignant sometimes, I couldn't tell if I was doing something right or something wrong. Mostly, we smiled and agreed with her. Julian and I had known for a long time that the universe didn't owe us shit. We didn't see a reason to point this out to our daughter too quickly.

I hadn't told my husband much about my time with Daniel, and I certainly didn't tell him that sometimes I still ached for him, ached for who he was as a boy and who I was as a girl. I also didn't know that much about Julian before he met me. I guess we didn't look to the past that much, but sometimes, when things were not going well with Julian, which was not often, I couldn't help but think that if Daniel and I could have held on, we might have had some kind of happiness.

I couldn't help but think of our daughter's vanished sibling. A sister, I was sure. A wisp of heart and hair, who said goodbye by way of a single, crimson streak of blood.

Sometimes I would wonder if our daughter Anastasia was the incarnate of the first; I would inhale and think maybe I really was very, very lucky and had two girls in one. She had enough brains for this to be true. The little sister keeping the bigger one, and sometimes I would think I knew which one was looking out at me, depending on whether her hazel eyes skewed blue or green.

•

I am not sure if it was him or me, but somewhere in the march of anniversaries, we leaned toward the traditional: paper, a bound diary and a desk set; cotton, three pairs of panties and a golf shirt; leather, a wallet and tasseled whip; silk, a smoking jacket and a handkerchief; wood, a jewelry box and a muddler;

wool, two scarves; bronze, a bracelet and a set of cufflinks.

At nine years, pottery, and we went to one of those studios where they give you a lesson and then let you paint your creation. Julian made a lopsided cup and I a lumpy plate. Then we had our respective coffee and toast from these on every day since.

It was easy for me to remember my vows, *in sickness, in health; for better, for worse.* I didn't mind the inevitability.

The days were long without my work. When Anastasia had been young, I had wished to stay at home with her, and while we could have maybe just made it work, by the time it seemed like a real possibility, she was old enough to already not need us so much anymore. At seven, she was mostly kinetic. We wondered what she would do next. Even as a baby she'd been the same, all wispy curls and potential.

I was happy to have time with her, but she was gone at school so much. I volunteered in her classroom to stay busy, I cooked meals for our family, I cleaned to a degree I did not know was possible. Sheets ironed twice a week, every pot scoured to a shine. I went through my closet, and then Julian's, and then Anastasia's. I called my mother, and I called Julian's mother. I did my best to stay occupied, but the projects were finite. I'd never thought of myself as someone so identified with work, but there I was, bored.

I mended our socks and replaced buttons because I had time.

I soaked beans for a meal and then cooked them because I had time.

I checked Anastasia's homework meticulously because I had time.

I discovered things I did not know, like my daughter's habits when she was just home from school—we'd let her sitter go—she would drop her backpack, kick off her shoes, and sit in the middle of the living room cross legged. She called this her *thinking time*, and her face was calm and focused. She had learned it in school. Afterward, at around ten minutes, she would hop up and require sustenance, half a jelly sandwich or some carrots.

I put in application after application, at other universities and schools, private enterprises, office manager jobs, anything really. There were some interviews, but it had been nearly a decade since I'd been on the market and things had changed, and I wasn't even that old yet. I wasn't prepared for all the questions, and I wasn't prepared for the competition. I had some panic, but Julian dismissed it. I said, *What if I never find another job!* And he said, *That actually sounds kind of nice.*

He was right then, hunched over his laptop. It probably did sound good, but I couldn't relax. I was doing my best, and he wasn't pushing. He wasn't the type of man who expected a wife who took care of everything, who laid out his clothes for the morning and made dinner and balanced the checkbook to the penny, but now he had one. There was no wrangling over who would pick up Anastasia and who would go to the store.

I would. Our household, mostly calm anyway, had a new peace about it—except for me.

I kept working at the applications, restructuring, rewriting, reformatting, refining my résumé and cover letter, but it always seemed the same: *Dear Hiring Manager* and *To Whom it May Concern*, and so much nothing back I wasn't sure what I was supposed to do.

It was hard to talk to him; my days had gotten more difficult, but Julian's had gotten easier, and we didn't need the money as much as I sometimes pretended. I asked him to look at my packet. I had him make me sample questions.

"What do you think of this shirt and skirt?" I asked once, on the way to one of the interviews that didn't give me an offer.

"You look fine," he said. "You look professional."

I smoothed my hair. The band of my pantyhose was cutting into my belly.

"But…" I said.

"It's not your outfits, I'm sure of it," Julian said. "The market is still tight."

"Maybe I should dye my hair," I said. "Maybe it would make me look younger."

"It's not your hair," he said. "Your hair is fine. Your hair is pretty."

"Thank you," I said.

There were times I'd lived on my own, sometimes in college, and after Daniel. There were in fact things I loved about my own space, like cleaning my piddly square footage in my underwear with a bottle of champagne, while the music played loud enough to wake the neighbors, or having tuna fish from the can over the sink for dinner—no hassle, no cleanup—but it wasn't everything. There were also the hard times, like being sick without anyone to go to the corner store, and the fact that one does not only bring home the bacon, but one cooks it and cleans up after it, alone. The bed is always cold, the morning coffee never made, though I finally had the sense to solve this problem with a timer. I hadn't remembered how hard it was to live this way until Julian and I got our first apartment together, which I resisted—even though things were going very well with him, it seemed like such a big step—and Daniel was still in my dreams, then, and still sometimes in the present.

Mostly, at night, it was dry lightning and fire.

I would be walking on a cowpath, single file in the skinny track, with Daniel just ahead. The slim shoulders of his frame as a child. The summer-blond hair. His gait, sure and steady ahead of me, and then the hillside would open, a bloom of red, like a wave gathered out of dirt and pine. Running, he would get farther and farther ahead of me. He had always been faster, but even with fear pushing me, I wasn't close to keeping up. A deer crossed the path, coat singed, antler smoking. And other animals, porcupines and bobcats, a quick moving bear, crowded the path. The cows too, clustered and lowing. Seedpods that had been waiting for the end of summer cracked open, the wind carried the flying varieties on their tiny parachutes. Tufts of milkweed clouded the air; I gasped trying to inhale. Daniel moved farther ahead. A moose, streaked in ash and dandelion, called for its mate. I wanted to collapse on the trail, but I kept going. A charcoaled grouse brushed my ankle, its wings clipped by flame. A badger, all snarl and snout, cruised low to the ground, groggy in the daylight but outpacing a pair of coyotes. I was overtaken by a gopher and a pack of field mice. When I inhaled, it was dust and hair and embers, and then I had to stop, in a choke of breath that wouldn't go down.

When the fire reached me, I put my head down to the earth, and thought of Daniel, far ahead of me now, the sounds of hooves and wings directly behind him, pushing him onward, headed for safety.

I did move in with Julian though, and in those days, I'd come home tired and cranky and sometimes the lights would be on and there would be something happening on the stove, or it would be Julian, tired and irritable, and I could say to him, *Here, I'll take your coat. There's wine open. Dinner in twenty.*

I tried to focus on how happy it was to know what one person could do for another. I was frustrated, but it was nice to dote on my husband, to make his egg, and make it perfectly, in the morning, to slide the just jelled yolk and nicely set white onto evenly browned and buttered bread. It was nice to spend the extra time with my daughter, to see how she changed every day.

I did dye my hair, bringing the brown up to a blonder shade of red, the color I'd been as a child, but I was trying to be frugal, and so I did it at home with Anne helping me, and the color came out splotched and uneven. I decided it didn't matter; the job applications were futile anyway.

Since I'd been a grocery clerk for a chain supermarket in college, I started filling out forms for big box stores, but even this industry had changed. At the group hiring meeting, my competition was younger, and stronger. I thought, *I have them beat on the drug test, I will nail the damn drug test,* and I did, but the union had been pushed out so no one cared about the years of experience I already had, and the jobs were paying less than ten years ago. I got an offer, but Julian said not to take it. He said if I started at minimum I'd have to start all the way over.

"Hold out," he said. "You're worth more."

•

It was Julian who suggested a vacation. Though I'd already been at home for several months, since we were savers, we had a little contingency fund that hadn't been touched in years.

"Just take a few weeks," he said a couple weeks after the New Year's party. He reminded me that first, before the gin ran out, before I'd been complacent and standing outside obsessed with the dog, I'd gotten rowdy and arranged penis shapes from baby carrots and radishes in the hummus dip, and then, after I had tired of it, I'd eaten every last crudité.

"That was a joke," I told him. It was from the grocery store years. "When I was at the store by campus, someone would come through at night and do up a zucchini and some kiwi in the ice case. It was funny."

"I know," Julian said. I could tell he did not think this was funny at all. "But maybe you need a break."

"What about Anne?" I asked.

"We can figure it out. We'll get her sitter back. I can work from home some days if I need to."

We looked online for cheap tickets. If I was going to do this, I wanted to go somewhere far, I wanted some distance, so I requested brochures and checked the consular warning pages. I narrowed my choices to Istanbul, Dublin, Paris, or Rome.

"Istanbul?" my mother asked when I spoke with her by phone. "Don't you think it's dangerous? I won't come there to claim your body," she said.

It was silly, mean even, but that's how I decided.

With something happening, the slow time started to move very quickly. I made casseroles to freeze. I packed and unpacked my bag several times. I called my friends and asked them to drop by and check in. I talked to my mother. I doted on Anne even more, to the point that she would push away from me sometimes, reminding me that I wasn't going to be gone forever. She was at the age where she rolled her eyes. I rolled mine back.

"I'll miss you," I said.

"I know," she said. "I *know*."

I left in mid-February on a long, multi-stop flight. Seattle, Chicago, Milan, Istanbul.

Each leg was a little more thrilling as I flew east. I had a sandwich in the Chicago airport, a double espresso in Milan. Breakfast was served on the flight as we zoomed toward Istanbul, a tiny plate of cheese and bread and cured sausage with a flyer that guaranteed the meat was free of pork.

By the time we touched down, I had been traveling for twenty-four hours and was dizzy with speed and pressurized air.

When I got off the plane and through the easy customs, I stopped at a change booth and exchanged my dollars for the local currency. Even an inexperienced traveler like me knew this was not necessarily the place to get the best rate, but I was here now. I wanted to be ready, and for a moment I worried that Julian might have been right—that beyond somewhere like an airport, there might be few services and a lot of dust.

Despite what the brochures said about the climate, I was convinced it would be warm—wasn't it the Middle East? Land of endless deserts and flies?—but it wasn't. Julian had implored me to bring cash, and to bring twice as much as I thought I'd need. He was practical. He said there might not be ATMs. It was a point of irritation. I had shown him the literature describing the country's amenities, and it was like he just didn't believe me—I guess it was the same way I didn't believe the climate—though I was glad for the sweater he'd forced me to pack.

I collected my lira, checked to make sure I had my things, examined the sticker in my passport, and headed for the exit doors.

The air whooshed around me and ushered me into chaos at the pickup area, large families wrangling jam-packed bags and herding their children, men smoking, women pushing children along the pitted sidewalk, horn after horn, the smell of diesel and something frying. There were some other tourists like me looking a little lost and overwhelmed, hair and faces greasy from their travel. The wind was blowing, just a little bit. I knew from the maps I had seen I was surrounded by water.

And it felt so familiar.

I knew, without question, I was passing through the double glass doors for the first time, yet I had heard other people describe a feeling similar to what I felt—an Italian-American colleague of mine, for example, when she stepped into Barcelona, where her parents were born, but a place that she'd never seen, felt at home. And I knew I had not ever seen this particular array of cars, nor had I seen these people in the streets or smelled the air carried to the gray curbside by these particular breezes.

And it took only a moment to see how wrong Julian was.

This place was cold and modern. They took Visa, MasterCard, and bribes.

It was late afternoon, and the taxicabs were flashing their brights at the crowd, trying to get the attention of potential fares.

I sat down on a bench. It was late morning. I thought I should look for a payphone to call Julian and Anne, but I waited. I went back inside and bought a pack of cigarettes from a kiosk. I smoked one, and then another, slowly.

There was something in that moment, surrounded by the men with their heavy mustaches and women in their heavy coats where—despite looking like an obvious tourist (my pale skin, my labeled luggage)—I first felt that I could just walk into the crowd and disappear.

It was the feeling of buoyancy. It was a feeling that the crowd would hold me, like water does, close on every part of the skin, and, with the tilt just right, I could float along indefinitely, instead of being swallowed whole.

I smelled the same briny air I'd gotten used to living in Seattle, but there was something underneath it, something that reminded me of the feeling of my father's hand resting lightly at the back of my neck when I was small, something that made me feel a sense of surety.

I hadn't brought much, a suitcase and my day-pack. I kept my things close as I sat on the bench and waited.

I remembered kissing Julian goodbye. I remembered how, when I went through the ropes and off toward the metal detectors, the TSA employee said to me, "You made that man cry," and I looked back at Julian, and he was indeed crying.

I was speechless. I hadn't seen him cry in years.

I'm not sure I had ever seen him cry for me.

I had an address for my hotel in the Sultan Ahmet area, a Mecca for tourists, and I finally got up and took a taxi there.

From the airport, there was nothing to see but high-rise apartment blocks stacked like layer cake and traffic. The buildings, all very similar, were poured from concrete, and the cars were a little boxier and smaller than American models; but mostly it was the mile after mile of houses piled in on top of one another and the buses and minibuses and more taxis and pedestrians and the minarets of the mosques that were stunning.

When I arrived at my hotel, I checked in without event. I was surprised when the man at the counter asked for my passport number, but he smiled through his beard and handed the document back quickly.

"There will not be hot water for another half an hour," he said. "We've just turned it on."

I went to my room, and the taps did, in fact, run cold. I would learn soon that this was common in countries where electricity was so expensive—tanks were simply switched off for most of the day, save for a few precious evening hours. I tested the bed, which was passable, and I opened my suitcase so the contents wouldn't be quite so smashed. I considered again that I should call Julian. I also considered that I wasn't sure if I could hear his voice yet, with trying to hear everything else around me.

Afternoon prayers had started and the call echoed off the stone tiles of my hotel.

I did not wash in the same way the faithful wash, from nostril to toe, but I freshened up in the cold water.

I was exhausted, but excited. I went back out into the street, and without my bags I felt light. I found an Internet café, and I wrote to my husband: *Flight was fine, but long. I'm in my hotel safely and getting ready to look for some early dinner or late lunch. I am not sure, exactly, how to make an international phone call, but once I've got it sorted I will ring.* I lied in that part—phone booths with a credit card swipe were plentiful. *Give Anne a hug for me, please. Love, Laura.*

I sent the email, paid, and then stopped at a kiosk built for tourists that sold postcards and stamps. I wrote a note to my daughter and handed it back to the boy in the stall—he had heavy eyebrows for someone so young and spoke perfect English. He promised he would drop the postcard in today's mail.

I took tea in a teahouse a few blocks down and wandered around the district.

Though there was a startling concentration of tourists like myself, it was not unlovely.

By evening prayer, I was rooted on a bench.

I had only seen pictures of such large mosques, and I had only heard the call to prayer, *ezan*, in newscasts. When the call begins, the voices of *imam* across the entire city start in with *Allahu akbar* (God is great), and from there, every *imam* puts his own twist on how the words are called, inventing the melody. Some are very good. They can sing the way we expect those called to the cloth should. Some are not so good, but Muslims listen anyway. Like Dylan almost—the notes don't ring, but it's the words that matter, it's the sentiment. When the mosques go off all at once, it is like the chatter of birds or children all speaking at once in a room, or an orchestra warming up. It's a cacophony, but it is holy.

I had never been a religious woman, but I listened to the call, and the voices did speak to me, saying,

Please, please. You have come so far, now come inside to pray.

•

For the first days I took taxis, indulging in the waste of cars after all my scrounging. All of the drivers near the tourist destinations spoke English. My hotel room was modest, and, even with hired cars and meals out and paying tourist prices, compared to what things cost in the US, I was not exactly burning through my lira. I packed up my daypack and spent my days out, visiting the museum homes of sultans and the ancient castles.

The week passed, easily. My plan had been to see some of Istanbul and then travel by bus to the interior of the country, come back, catch my flight, go home perhaps tired but renewed. I think Julian's expectation was that, on return, I would get interested again: get more serious about figuring out what was going wrong in my job search, commute if I had to, or do more with my days than cooking and braiding Anne's hair.

For tourist destinations, I had meant to head inland, but I delayed.

The city was fascinating, and I grew bolder and bolder, taking the minibuses, then taking the city buses. I had a guidebook, and I went to the points in it, and then I went beyond, walking through crowded and empty alleys, dipping into cheese shops and teahouses. I bought a scarf and covered my hair to see how it would feel. No one looked at me any differently, but I felt like I was in disguise.

I worshipped some. Not formally, but as close as I'd ever gotten. Even in just a few days, with my body turned sideways from jet lag, I felt looped into the *ezan*. I would wait for it, listen for it, pay attention to it when it came. I hadn't yet gotten the courage to go into a mosque, except into the large ones that were attractions, and I wasn't sure of the gender customs—I knew Friday was off-limits, but that was all. Still, I kept my ears open for the *imam*, and my heart.

I visited the Internet café again and wrote to Julian. *It is hard for me to describe what I am seeing here. On the one hand, this is a normal, modern city. It is the kind of place where you can certainly get whacked by the commuter train. On the other hand, it's not like visiting Austin, which is different from Seattle but not foreign. It's different than visiting London, which is foreign but lacking this kind of shimmer. So far, I have not left Istanbul. Will call soon, Laura.*

When Julian wrote back, he said, *We are fine here. Don't worry about the expense of a call, it is enough for us to know you are having fun and you are safe. Anne got your postcard.*

I was surprised at the speed of the mail, but I wasn't sure I was safe.

At a week, the constipation from new food and the dehydration from travel turned from uncomfortable to actual illness. I hadn't been so sick since I was a child. I spent most of the evening vomiting into the recessed toilet, and then, though my period wasn't due, I started bleeding, and it wouldn't stop.

For three days I was down in what became the greasy linens of the hotel bed. I could not remember feeling so helpless as an adult. In the fever, I felt very, very alone. The hotel staff brought me mineral water with aspirin dropped into it, a supposed remedy for bowel trouble, and kept the windows locked tight. Heat choked the room, and I did feel like something was burning out of my body, though I could not have said what it was.

On the fourth day, I awoke out of the haze. I took cheese and bread with salted tomatoes for breakfast. The hotel proprietor's daughter brought me tea in my room, quietly, with her head down.

It wasn't until after that I remembered that during the whole time, I hadn't called anyone from the hotel—they'd simply noticed that I'd entered my room and not left, and I felt sudden gratitude, followed by a deep indignation; it was not the kind of kindness, I figured, that would ever happen in an American establishment. First of all, if anyone noticed a guest had retired semi-permanently, the most investigating that might happen would be some banging on the door and a hollered reminder about checkout. And second, maybe not even that.

When I am honest, I know that I had traveler's sickness. Or maybe a touch of what I had heard called the meat sickness—a bad reaction to the different bacteria in animal products from a geography that is not your home. Americans, with such sanitary supermarkets, are susceptible to this especially. So I was sick with that or something else, stressed, and trying to let go of the feeling of fever.

When I am honest, I also know my body was becoming clean, as if pulling out the silt when panning for gold.

Waking from a fever is almost like venturing outside after heavy rain or a quick fire, when the air is still a little heavy and the eyes smart from the light.

And the world has been washed or the underbrush burned clear.

On the other side of the world, the moon and the stars seemed in the wrong place, the gravity different, and it was as if the tether that had held me to my life in Seattle had come undone somewhere between being racked with fever and chills, and now, emptied, I could just float off into the mist above the minarets that punctured the skyline.

After my breakfast, I dressed in my only sweater because I still had some of the chills of nausea, and the wind coming off the Bosporus cut my skin. Boarding a bus headed toward Taksim, the city's historical center, I had the kind of lucidity that the ill are sometimes granted—my life sketched on vellum and laid overtop the Puget Sound and then, just as easily, across the Golden Horn.

I got off the bus in Taksim's main square and chose from one of the towering lunch shops flanking the street.

Bread.

Salt.

Water.

I thought, *Maybe there's nothing else.*

I took my tea quietly, sitting on the low wooden stool. I ate my *simit*, a firm dough baked circular, covered with sesame.

My hands had gotten ragged, and I felt fatigue around my eyes. The cashier near me was moving very quickly. I sat near a window opening onto the street, and the customers zoomed in and out. Traffic streamed like time-elapsed film. After the slow lull of illness, the entire world around me moved so fast.

When I thought of America, the bread crumbled in my mouth like ash.

•

It was sudden. I had only a day of my two weeks left; my flight would embark in the morning. I'd spent most of my time touristing, sick, or frantically searching for toilets. I had still not heard my family's voices.

I had walked through the old Byzantine cisterns and seen the pillars that stood on Medusa heads.

I had walked barefoot through Mimar Sinan's mosques.

I had had my shoes shined by a seven-year-old on the street.

Dutifully, I had checked my email and written to Julian those few times when I wasn't ill. I had gorged myself on meatballs and tahini and things I wasn't sure there were English names for, but I felt thinner. Light. I was beginning to understand the pace of the city, its ancient sprawl. I had stopped noticing the damp cold, shirked the paranoia about bag snatchers and pickpockets.

Finally, my body settled, and so did I.

I could breathe, and the air was damp and salty, like a lover.

I spent my final hours in a fish house on the Black Sea, staring into a glass of *rakı*, an alcohol I understood women did not ordinarily drink in public but had been served to me because I was clearly foreign.

The fish house was dark, with waxy tablecloths, rough wooden furniture, and dirty windows looking onto the water. The waiter served my drink in two parts—ice water in a fluted glass, the small bottle of transparent liquor set beside it. Mixed, the liquid turned pearl. Turks called it *aslan sütü*, lion's milk, and I sipped mine slowly, waiting for the surge of courage or at least drunken impulsiveness.

There was nothing. The fish house started to close its doors, and the only light were the candles on the tables. I smelled coal. I was not exactly sure which buses I had taken to get here, as it had been day then, and I'd followed a sort of general, weaving path. I settled the tab and stepped into the dim cold.

I had enough cash on me, maybe, for a cab, depending on how far I'd really come. It was very late, but my head was finally starting to turn, like someone had just greased up the gears and got the whole machine moving. I counted my bills again. I wandered, a little drunk, until I found a storefront with an ATM, and I withdrew as much as it would let me. I hailed a taxi.

"Sultan Ahmet," I told the driver, feeling sure, feeling clear, feeling loose, finally.

•

In the morning, I felt it was only fair to at least make an attempt.

I took my packed bags and got on the metro. The seats were sculpted in garish orange plastic. I sat near one of the car doors. I rode the train to the end of the line, the airport stop. My flight would leave in three hours, at 9:57 a.m.

But I did not get off, couldn't get off, so instead I rode the length of the tracks, back to the starting point at Sirkeci, and then back to the airport, where again I watched the passengers file out, and I stayed put.

I rode the train until my flight would have been well in the air.

It was like establishing an alibi.

Hours later, I dragged my bag onto the train platform and across the cobbles and back to the hotel. I hadn't even bothered to check out, though I didn't process it until I returned, and the proprietor looked my luggage up and down but didn't comment. I talked with him and negotiated one more night's stay and then walked around the corner to a payphone to call my youngest brother in Bismarck. It was extremely early in the morning in North Dakota, and he didn't even know I was in Istanbul, but had always been solid and promised to relay a message to Julian and my parents. *Tell them I missed my flight, and I will be in touch soon, I said. Tell them I'm sorry. Try to call before Julian goes to the air-port to pick me up, but there's ten hours until then; you have time.*

He must have been wondering why I didn't call Julian myself, but he didn't ask.

"Okay, Laura," he said. "Are you okay?"

"I think so," I said. The telephone had a digital counter on it. I wasn't sure if it was calculating the time or the cost of the call.

"Do you need me to come get you?" he asked. "Are you getting on the next flight?"

"Richard, do you even have a passport?" I asked.

"Do I need one?" he asked.

"Yes," I said. "You need one."

"I could get one," he said. "I would get one."

"I know you would."

For the rest of the day, I wandered. I wasn't sure what I was doing, but it felt important. I bought another postcard and wrote a note to Anastasia. *You are an amazing daughter and I love you.* I gave it to the same young man with the heavy eyebrows who worked the kiosk. I wondered what other people wrote, and I wondered how many of the messages the cashier read.

I had lunch in a pretty café on the water, meatballs and peppers and tomatoes, and I thought about the money I had. I thought about my credit card in the payphone, time stamping me. Julian would see it on the statement.

When Richard called him—maybe Richard had already called—Julian would ring my hotel. He had the information.

He would send me an email, which I could decide to read or not read. I didn't have a mobile, then.

I thought of my family, my tidy life. It had become only a little unraveled by losing my job, but I felt it fraying now, like one thread picked from a seam.

My mother used to tell me to snip those, instead of tugging.

I promised myself I would go back. I promised myself I would keep writing postcards, for now. I promised myself I would call Julian, soon, but I felt drawn, and like nothing I'd ever experienced before, a clear feeling that there was something I needed to find out, and that it was here in this place that I'd chosen mostly because my mother hadn't liked the idea of it.

I closed my eyes.

I pulled.

When I got back to my room, the man at the desk said there had been a phone call.

"Urgent, miss," he said, and handed me a folded scrap of paper. My home phone line was written on it, and my husband's name, spelled the Turkish way, *Culian.*

I slept hard that night, and for the first time in a long time, I had the Daniel dream, but in this version he grabbed my hand and pulled me along with him, the beasts and birds thundering along with us, and we gained speed even as the cowpath turned rocky and snaked up a hill in a series of switchbacks. I didn't know where we were going. I had never seen this stretch of trail before, and it felt like we were moving toward the fire instead of away from it, but I kept with the pack anyway. I could see we were headed for a ridge, and we scrambled through loose dirt and underbrush—Daniel's feet moved so fast he hardly touched ground, and I was light alongside of him. The ridge was a huge outcropping of rock, and then I saw there must be caves there, where we could burrow deep inside, a cool jaw opening from the earth. We ducked under the first eave of rock, the space suddenly close with the other creatures crowding in behind us. We careened downward. The squawking and braying quieted some in the dark.

"Ahead," Daniel said, "we'll have to jump." He was breathing hard.

A torch had appeared; it smelled of horsehair and pine tar. Funny, this bit of welcome fire.

We ran some more, along a ridge, the animals at full gallop behind us, all following Daniel. And the place, a gap. We could see where the route picked up on the other side, but it seemed very wide. I wasn't sure we could make it.

"We can," Daniel said. His face was streaked with sweat and soot. He seemed so sure when we backed up as far as we could, leaning into the coats of the creatures, smoky dander and still some seedpods clinging, to get a run at it.

And we launched into the inky air.

Pull.

•

The next day I took a blanket from the hotel and dragged most of my luggage to the streets near the train stop. There had been a constant, informal bazaar taking place, so I joined in. I laid my clothes out and sold the majority of them to Turks and some to

European tourists: American brands I had paid too much for and mostly not worn since leaving home.

I shared a sly smile with the other pavement vendors, hawking their stolen Adidas and knock off Louis Vuitton handbags. I took whatever buyers offered. I kept only my toilet things, all of the jewelry I was wearing and the few other pieces I had brought, and my daypack. The jewelry could fetch more money than any of the clothes, but I wanted metal next to my skin, not softness.

I had held softness for far too long.

•

With my luggage reduced to what my faded blue daypack could hold, the feeling of lightness was less abstract. *Everything I have*, I thought, *it fits here*. So neatly. A few changes of underwear, a clean shirt, a nice wool sweater, canvas pants, socks. A tangle of silver at the bottom and my guidebook.

I wasn't sure what I was doing, but I knew my money wouldn't last in a city, so I checked out of the hotel for good. I took the orange train to the inter-city bus station, a building made of mirrored glass, and I bought a ticket from a man at the counter. I intended to see the interior of the country after all.

"One?" he asked me.

"Yes," I said.

"One?" he asked again.

"Yes," I said.

"One woman," he said. He pecked at an ancient computer and a ticket growled from his printer.

He gave me a seat in front, directly behind the driver. I kept my daypack with me instead of putting it into the cargo space in the low belly of the vehicle, and climbed into my seat. The bus was clean and wide like a hallway. It had been too long, I thought, since I had thought of myself as one, singular, the solitaire stone in a silver setting, the remaining finger on a millworker's hand.

I wondered about Julian, about Anne, and I will admit that in the first steps I took after I'd purchased my ticket, I faltered some in thinking of them.

Their faces were still clear to me. I could hear Anne's voice—*You coming back soon?*—and I could hear my own voice in answer to her. I knew I should call Julian immediately. He'd really never asked me to play the wife to him—never had he tried to use authority or pressure to make me change my mind, but I worried if I called now, he might, and I never wanted to hear him talk that way to me, to anyone. To implore or to demand or worse, to beg. When he asked me to marry him, he said, *I want to spend the rest of my life with you,* and I said, *So do it,* and he said, *Marry me,* and I said, *Okay.* Never as a question, just a conversation we'd had that decided something. I liked that about him. So I couldn't call.

I boarded the bus, seat one. *One.*

CHAPTER TWO

When I left Istanbul on the bus that cruised gently from the coast into the heart of Anatolia, I had, like torn halves of the same snapshot, a memory. First, a cobbler hammering small heels onto little girls' dress shoes, and each was painted chrome. He sat on a low three-legged stool, and the pile of shoe crowded around him and overflowed out of his door and into the street, like spawning fish into a causeway. Second, nearby, in the tiny yard of a tumbledown house, a Turkish-made car, the finish oxidized and tires gone flat, was for sale, and heaped inside were the tanks of four or five Western toilets, broken into pieces.

I saw these things while walking through a neighborhood I didn't know and definitely didn't know the name of. I was just walking. Not for exercise, not to go somewhere, just passing time until my bus left.

And then, while I rode, sunken into the upholstery, head against the window, I thought of the shoes and the car to stay focused—the cobbler, pounding away, the car, static. The air had been clear and the street softly shaded, and I worked very hard at keeping myself at the center of the picture. My daughter would have been thrilled at the shape and the quantity of the shoes; my husband would have had something more precise for me: *not fish*, he'd say, *herring. They fish them in Alaska for roe, now that all the salmon are gone.*

But I didn't think this way, and I didn't think how they both would have given the same puzzled face at the car, how she might have kicked at one of the tires, how he might have swiped a finger across the bumper to test the depth of the dirt. Instead, I remembered only the hammer against the silver heels, and the white of the porcelain through the dusty rear window. I thought of only myself on the patched cobbles of the street and distracted myself trying to come up with some of the words from my small Turkish dictionary. *Araba*, car. *Ayakkabi*, shoe. *Beni*, me. *Balik*, fish. *Pencere*, window.

I was very tired and I didn't know the word for it—the two weeks I'd been in this country hadn't necessitated learning verbs—but when the bus stopped for breaks, and also when the porter came around with the beverage tray, I tried to revive myself. Tea with sugar. Coke. Sweetened coffee. Bites of chocolate. I felt sleep falling onto me. I wanted to stay awake for this—this exit. I'd come to Istanbul as a solo tourist, and I was leaving as someone else, having purposefully missed my flight, counted my remaining money, and purchased a bus ticket that sent me spinning twelve hours east into West Asia.

In the morning I clomped off the bus. I was still pretending some. I had chosen the small town from my guidebook in part for its scenery, and for its quality as a destination for sightseers. As the others tripped out of their seats, I was grateful, when I saw the weight of their suitcases and travel bags, that I had only my blue daypack. I weaved my way out of the small crowd that had formed around us—hotel owners and taxi drivers petitioning a new crop of vacationers—and into the shelter of a stone building. I smoked a cigarette. It was still cold, the first of March. The cigarette offered me no warmth, and after a few drags I stomped it out.

I looked for a kiosk and purchased a postcard.

Like a trail of breadcrumbs.

The landscape was like nothing I'd ever seen— columns of red, yellow, tan, pink rock with caps of gray. It was like being in a cave except there was wide, open sky. I'd read in my guidebook that villagers had carved out the columns and lived in them, a castle for one, and before that, the ancient people had excavated underground cities out of the soft rock that later was home to persecuted Christians.

I wasn't sure I could actually stay. It was exactly the sort of place to look for a missing tourist. There must have been caches of them like the Piper's children, somewhere in the farther reaches, in the places missed by preservation societies, holed up in the dark with a store of dried apricots and oranges. I imagined there *had* to be, there *must* be a band of the disappeared—but for the time being, I needed a bed.

I wondered how long it would take Julian to hop on a plane and come looking. I remembered registering at the embassy when I had thought I was only going on vacation. Address on file, emergency contact information. I wondered if they would do anything, if my visa expired.

I started walking. I felt like I could walk forever, weaving through the cramped houses and curling alleyways. I stopped for breakfast and had coffee and cheese and bread.

Yasemin was my first sign of luck. In our chat, I learned she was a village woman; she'd taken over a twenty-room guesthouse when the former owner moved to Germany. The place was off the main roads some, but there were pretty hand-painted signs pointing to it. It was more English than I'd spoken in weeks. Her rooms were small and clean, and some of them were shared bunks for budgeting backpackers. All told, Yasemin could hold around twenty-five people, more if there were couples that didn't mind spooning all night to fit the twin mattresses.

I stayed with her three nights before I decided to propose a trade. In the day, I wandered through the town, stumbling in the remaining cold. Spring came late here, sandwiched in the valleys in the shadow of a volcanic range.

Three nights passed, splayed out under her blankets, or curled into a ball, before I really realized where I was.

My husband had received my message, but had he understood?

I wondered if I should call my brother again.

And I watched Yasemin, somewhere in her forties, crash about her hotel in slippers that clacked against the soles of her feet, wearing a baggy village skirt, the center of it, at the bottom, hand-stitched together to make almost-trousers. She covered her hair with a simple cotton scarf.

Under my breath I sang a Leonard Cohen song to myself.

I tried to leave you, I don't deny…

The real tourist season had not yet started, and on the morning after the third night, Yasemin invited me for tea in her courtyard. She had wrapped herself up in a heavy blanket, and she gave one to me. We sat there as I smoked, and we talked about the town some, what I had seen. We talked about the hotel. She asked if my room was satisfactory, and if I still planned to stay for a week.

"I think longer," I said. "Maybe you need a helper? For board only? I can cook and I'm handy."

"Handy?" she asked.

"I mean I am all right at fixing things."

"Are you seeing some things which need to be fixed?"

"No," I said.

We sat in her white plastic chairs, thoughtfully looking at the new green budding on her terrace plants.

"Then how long will you stay?" she asked.

"I don't know," I said, and I felt the relief pool around me like the cobbler's shoes to have admitted it.

She took a cigarette from my pack and I lit it for her.

"Sure," she said, exhaling. "We deal. You work, you eat, you sleep free."

I smiled at her.

"But you work," she repeated.

Maybe people who have been desperate recognize the look on others' faces. Maybe she was truly kind. Or lonely.

"If the season is not good, there will be no more pay than this," and she swept her hand across the courtyard for emphasis.

We looked around at the plants again. I couldn't think of anything I would need money for, yet, and she was so cautious. I tried to shake her hand, and she leaned in and kissed me, once on each cheek, and we smiled at each other, each having shared a secret; me, displacement; her, economics. And now we were friends, like two girls at a new school.

The next day, my fourth among the rocky Cappadocian landscape, she beat on my door before the sun was up full. We cleaned every room from the ceiling to the floor, scrubbing the painted walls, smacking the carpets, scouring toilets and sinks and basins.

The rooms, though, were already clean, most having spent the night empty.

Yasemin's place was nearly vacant, and it would, except for a few roaring days, stay that way. She cleaned the rooms from habit, almost in ritual, and I learned to do the same.

Iron the sheets twice to keep time from wrinkling and turning in.

Tend the potted plants instead of yourself.

Dry the cutlery to a shine, but don't look at the reflection.

I was inefficient in her kitchen. The hotel offered complementary breakfast and dinner for a pittance, so we chopped potatoes into perfect cubes, boiled water on the low heat, and practiced making Turkish coffee, of which every cup Yasemin tasted and promptly spit out.

"You'll never find a husband," she told me.

I kept my silence.

She smiled. She showed me again how to wash rice. Showed me again how to cull the cereal grains and wash off the talc used for polishing.

She showed me she had her own secrets and how she kept them, folded inside her dishcloths and dolmas.

My days were punctuated by her repetitive, often unneeded labor. Yet, while I could see that there was no real sense of urgency—the rugs we'd beaten yesterday, we would beat again today, and in the meantime, no one would tread across them—I think for both of us there was reason enough not to let our hands get idle.

I was not sleeping well. Still, as tired as I was, I was grateful to have something to do all day. Sometimes, in the afternoons, she'd check the bus schedule, and satisfied no tourists would arrive for an hour or so, she'd take me walking through the fields and across the talus. I wasn't sure, exactly, what made me stick there, other than having no other place to go. And Yasemin, steady and reliable as a metronome, compelled me.

I thought of my daughter. I wondered how Julian was explaining my delay to her. At the kiosk I wrote another postcard.

Dear Anastasia,

The landscape here is very pretty. I wish you were with me.

Love,

Mom.

Friday mornings Yasemin allowed me to sleep in. Allowed. I was maybe ten years her junior, but a grown woman all the same. She prayed in her room. I tried to capture some of the sleep that eluded me.

"I will ask *Allah* to help you dream," she said.

I tipped my head in thanks, but I wasn't sure I wanted this.

So far, nothing had arrived for me. No letters, no agents of the government. Almost every day, walking, I passed an Internet café and I turned my head. *Julian*, I thought, *I'm sorry*. Perhaps I was negligent to my daughter. Perhaps I relied too much on thinking that he would take care of her.

The village was small, with spires of soft rock topped with volcanic basalts sprouting from the ground like the first uneven shoots in a bean patch, and though we were still strangers, I think Yasemin was as happy for my company as I was for hers. There were not many guests, and most of the people who did come through were local travelers. So, if I were in the front reception area, if I heard shoes at the door, I would look up immediately. Soles on the tile are an odd sound, anyway, in places where the local custom is to be barefoot indoors.

Late afternoon on a Friday, I watched a man lope into the courtyard and sit down to smoke before he decided if he wanted to stay. I'd seen him around in the village before, taking photographs. Clearly, a *yabancı*—a foreigner to Turkey—but just as clearly, not a tourist. Tourists have a look about them; they look hungry or confused, or they smoke brands of cigarettes that are extremely expensive locally, or they have backpacks that don't look all the way worn in.

I met him in the lobby with my eyes down like a village woman would. I wore some of my jewelry, earrings and a thick bracelet. Even my glasses felt a little shiny, hooked behind my ears. I liked the way that the silver and chrome reflected off my freckles, and I liked the hardness of these tones against my fair skin and the sureness of the firm shape of metal.

I took his ID—the government mandated that foreign hotel guests have their passport number recorded—thick with extra pages and ratty stamps. His passport was navy blue and printed with the spread gold eagle, like mine. His name was Paul, but I couldn't place his accent, and I finally looked up and asked him where he was from, originally.

"California," he said.

I must have raised my eyebrow. "The Golden State," I said.

He had gaps between his teeth and was unshaven. Brown eyes, a little slope to his back.

"They say that," he said. "I haven't been there in awhile." He looked away from me, out at the rock, out at Yasemin's pretty terraces, out past the late winter puddles and the outline of Mount Erciyes, the local volcano.

He was staring at me.

He was stuffing his identification back into his tan shoulder bag.

He was turning to walk out as Yasemin came through the side door.

"He's been here before," she said. "He must live somewhere near. Maybe Kayseri or Nevşehır," she added. "Definitely expat." She straightened the desk. She looked me in the eye.

My first working day, Yasemin had told me that she didn't particularly like renting rooms to traveling expats. She thought of them as people with no clear sense of home; she did not trust the impulse to run, and so she preferred vacationing Turks or proper tourists. I wasn't sure if she was right, but I understood her. She compared it to taking a clipping of a plant. First, when the clipping is in water, it will put out roots. But most cuttings, she said, will not bloom without some earth of their own to sink into.

I thought that there's also something to changing the arrangement of the garden, or putting new dirt in an old pot, or creating a successful graft that will green up the leaves, make the blossoms come in full, or help the fruit to survive a frost.

I think Yasemin did not associate me as a fugitive yet.

"He doesn't have a ring," Yasemin said to me.

"No," I said. But then, neither did I. Mine was stashed in an envelope beneath the mattress in my room.

"He is handsome for an American, no?"

"He looks very much like people I know."

"*Hahhh*," she said, the Turkish way of saying *I see*. "He is like you."

"Yes," I said, but that wasn't it. It was more than a common face. I meant that if she were right about expats, maybe I was like him.

•

Every other week, Yasemin would make the forty-five minute bus trip to the town of Kayseri to go to the bigger supermarkets and also just to get out. It wasn't the closest place to shop, but she said there were better deals, and Kayseri people loved to haggle. She said that if I were going to be her helper, I would have to come along.

As we traveled east, Mount Erciyes came more into focus. The Greek geographer Strabo wrote that the volcano was never free from snow in his lifetime, and that those who ascended it could see both the Black Sea and the Mediterranean. When I hung out the daily wash to flap in the wind, the peak was something static to fix on. The washing was one of my chores, every morning. I did it by hand.

When we arrived in Kayseri, we transferred to a local bus, traveling through the downtown with its statues of Atatürk, some historic Selçuk era tombs—one of them functioning as a roundabout—and high-rise apartment buildings poured in solid concrete and painted in pastels, white lace curtains in every window.

Yasemin ducked into a fabric shop, and I stayed on the street to smoke and look for a kiosk to buy a stamped postcard. It would be good to send Anne things from different places, I thought. The smoking was a habit I had been casual about for years, but I had re-adopted it in full, being in a place where no one seemed to care about it one way or the other.

So far, I liked working for her, even if it was more about keeping busy and keeping quiet. I had some money, but I wanted it to last, and I knew that at some point the cash I'd come with would trickle out, and I'd find something I would not be able to barter my time for—like the hospital, or a renewed visa. I dreaded the day when the smooth slide of my bank card would stamp my location on a statement, colder and surer than the postcards.

Away from my life, I'd found I was less content with it than I had thought.

Away from my life, I'd seen a chance to make a new one.

I peeked through the window and watched Yasemin deal with the shopkeeper, flirting with him in the subtle, practiced way she must have learned in the village, smiling while she looked past him, turning so he could see the slope of her bottom, turning back to show the round of her breast, but almost imperceptibly. If I was right about her age, she looked it, but her eyes were electric, as dark as hazelnut. She was not married, and so she wore no ring, but her fingers, I thought, were perfect. Short nails, cuticles a little ragged, round knuckles—it was clear that, like everyone else in the village, Yasemin labored. Even with her loose-fitting, drab country clothes, and her barely noticeable angling, on our errands, I had yet to see a man tell Yasemin no. She was older than I was, but she was much more beautiful.

I was running out of things to write on Anne's postcards, considering I wasn't really saying anything to her about what I was doing or when I would be back. I decided on, *I miss you, I wish you were here*, because these things were true.

"Hello," I heard.

The thing I had already realized about Kayseri was that if you forgot for one moment, it was easy to imagine that it was anywhere. Home to a mid-sized university, a sugar refinery, and a small military base, Kayseri also had Western fast food, people with gray faces, and masses of unhappy-looking young.

And this man, from the boardinghouse.

"Hi," I said. We did a proper introduction. His name was Paul, I remembered that from his passport.

"What are you doing in Kayseri?" he asked.

"Shopping," I said. "You?"

"I live here. My wife teaches at the university. Have you been to the sausage shops? Kayseri is famous for sausage," he said.

"No," I said.

"Well, listen," he said, "I'm glad I saw you. I've been trying to organize a trip up Erciyes, and no one wants to go. Just for the day. While there's still some snow."

"Yeah," I said, "Okay." *Why not*, I thought. March had stayed chilly; the spring came slow around the base of the mountain.

Then, he said he was running late, and he walked off briskly. I kept one eye on him, his light hair bobbing half a head above the crowd.

When Yasemin came out to the street, she handed me a parcel wrapped in brown tissue. "For your room," she said. "To make new curtains."

I tore at the edge of the package a little, and underneath there was a splash of spangled orange.

"I love orange," I told her.

"You can use some color," she said. She waited and looked at me. "What did he want, Laura?"

I liked the way she said my name, not skipping any of the vowels.

"To go up the mountain," I said.

"Erciyes?" she said, her pitch sloping. "*Allah-hallah*. If an idea comes to an American's head they think it must be a good one. I think it is healthier to stay put."

I laughed because I wasn't sure what to say.

"Be careful." She said this tenderly, as I cradled the fabric she'd bought for me, and I thought of Paul, disappearing down the long, busy street.

•

At night it felt like Yasemin's prayers had worked, and dreaming came in full, sometimes, just long swaths of nonsense, and sometimes stretches of lucidity: the smell of my daughter's shampoo—she liked a drugstore brand that was bubblegum and coconut, Julian hated it, but I hoped he remembered to buy it for her anyway—the scratch of my husband's chin against my neck in the morning, when he was stubbled and still half asleep, and sometimes I could talk him into letting me crawl on top of him for a minute. He would be very quiet, turning his face away. I wondered if he was thinking of his email, or of another woman. It didn't matter. I was happy to be close to him, even if he looked like he wanted to be somewhere else.

Even if we both did.

I woke one night from what I thought was the beginning of a Daniel dream—all I knew was heat and my feet hitting rock.

My room was clean and cold, but I was hot under a heavy quilt, sweating. I got up and checked my face in the mirror. I was the same person, just displaced, confused. I thought of packing the entire knapsack, but I took only my credit card.

The town was very dark. There was one bar that catered to tourists, blaring American Top 40 songs, though there was hardly anyone filling the seats. The season was slow for everyone, not just Yasemin.

There was a phone booth in the town square, and it was as empty as everywhere else. I swiped my card and the box lit up. I dialed—I hardly had to look at the numbers, we'd had the same number for so long.

It was March second. A month had passed since I'd left Seattle.

It was my daughter who answered—her voice was perfect, even thousands of miles away.

"Anne," I said. It was morning there. "Are you on your way to school?"

"Yes," she said. I heard her cover the receiver and call for her father.

"Anne," I said, "I miss you."

Julian had the phone now. I could hear Anastasia in the background. *Tell her, tell her, tell her,* she said.

"Laura, I have to ask you if you are safe," Julian said.

My practical husband. My daughter, a better image of us both.

"Very," I said. "I am in no danger."

"Damn you," he said. *Tell her!* What sounded like a plate or a cup dropped. "You need to get on a plane, immediately."

I hadn't thought about this much, I realized. What I would say. What I would offer.

"You know I have tickets. I was coming to look for you, the consulate won't do shit."

"I don't know what they can do," I said, though I had wondered.

"Me neither," he said, and then, muffling the handset, "Anne, go into the living room."

My head turned over. He was coming?

"When are you coming, Jules?"

"Next week. Unless you tell me I don't need to. I know it was crappy lately for you here, but I'm coming to that town you've been posting from, and I am taking you back. Your mother is coming here to watch Anne."

I will admit I liked the fire in his voice. I hadn't heard it in a long time.

"Julian," I said. "Don't come. I'm not ready yet."

I heard him breathe. I heard him think, *Goddamn you.* I heard him start to pick up whatever had dropped.

"Okay," he said. I heard deep breath. "Okay. Talk to your daughter then. She wants you back."

He put Anastasia back on the line, and I thought she sounded a little nervous as we chatted, but I talked to her slowly, so the delay wouldn't make an echo.

Yes, school was going well. *Yes*, being with just Daddy was okay. *Yes*, she missed me, too. *Yes*, she was excited to see Grandma.

"Anne," I said. "I think this is probably very hard for you, but I promise I will come home."

"I know, momma," she said. "But I don't like waiting."

When I depressed the phone into the cradle, the stars were full in the sky, and there was a swirl of dust coming up from the road. I was very tired. The bar was letting out and there were a few drunken tourists swaying in the street. Slowly, I made my way back to Yasemin's, my daughter's voice in my head.

I knew she couldn't understand everything, but I hoped she would understand a little.

•

A week after the shopping trip, Yasemin and I were making the curtains. She was surprised I could sew, and we laughed as she tried to teach me some Turkish while I worked her old machine. The season seemed perpetually slow, but we set up in the lobby just in case someone came by. She gave me some words to try and memorize, and then she quizzed me.

"Thread," she said.

"*Iplik!*" I flicked the presser foot tight against the fabric.

"To sew," she said.

"*Dikmek!*" I went forward and then reversed the direction of the stitch to make a knot.

"Bobbin," she said.

"*Makara!*" I depressed the foot pedal deeply and zipped out a quick, even seam. When I had been learning to sew, I used to get frustrated as my mother was teaching me. I would say, *This isn't really sewing. It's all pinning and ironing.* And she would tell me, *You're right. It's the difference between something looking homemade and professional.*

I never became a good seamstress, but I did get good enough that when I wanted to I could make nice baby quilts for friends, take in a pair of trousers, or mend rips even if they were off the seam. She was right that it was about the patience.

I liked working with the bright, fluid cloth Yasemin had picked out. It was like shaping flame.

When the door tapped open, I stopped so quickly the tension on the machine kicked back and spooled the thread into a wad.

"Hello," Paul said. "Don't let me interrupt your lessons."

How was my face then? I was shy, suddenly, that he'd heard my attempts at domestic Turkish.

"Not at all," I said. I looked at where the needle had jumped.

Yasemin said something I didn't understand.

"*Tamam,*" he said. *Okay.*

He asked if I wanted to have tea with him, and she waved us both out of the room then.

I think she saw more than I saw. At the teahouse, Paul and I sat on the low stools and watched a few tourists filter in and out. The first teas I had in Turkey seemed so strong, even when I took them with sugar. Now, I was happily drinking tea black.

Paul told me that he was on a collecting mission. He was a sculptor. Or something of a sculptor—he fused rocks and wood and made abstract art.

"I have a show coming up in Kayseri," he said.

"I thought we were planning a mountain trip."

"I am," he said. "But the soonest will be a day or two after my show."

When we came back from tea, I could see the flash of orange in my room's window where Yasemin had finished and hung the curtains. I hoped she had noticed that I kept the place tidy, that the bed was made, and my few clothes folded. I felt soft for her. Who was this woman who had taken me in, who did nothing but try to make my life more beautiful?

I turned to Paul in the courtyard. "What did she say to you before we left?"

He raised an eyebrow and shook his head. "You'll have to practice your Turkish more," he said.

I looked at the curtains again as I thought of Yasemin's sweetness.

Paul stayed at the hotel two more nights, and I saw him each day. We drank tea and talked. He had dirt around his cuticles from scavenging in the hillsides. He had a shine in his eye.

•

The next week, I did go to Kayseri to see Paul's show. Along with the rocks and sticks he'd collected, he had incorporated parts of the cultural landscape: a rack of beef rib not quite picked clean—which by the end, he reported, started stinking. A jug of *ağda*—a mixture of honey and wax women used to strip their bodies clean of hair—suspended between some boards and drizzling a thread of gold into a cone of sand.

The bus ride seemed longer without Yasemin, and Kayseri seemed grayer. I knew people had been there for centuries, but I didn't get the sense of a great history. It seemed like toil to me. Hundreds of years of trying to get by. Hundreds of years of walks to the *tekel* (the state-run liquor stores), to the brothels, and through winter storms, which Yasemin said were cold enough to keep even the wild dogs away.

It seemed perfect and disheartening that Paul lived in this place.

I had learned from our chats his wife worked long hours at the university, and he put in long hours with his own private students and his installations, and they came home and prepared the spare, basic meals they preferred. He had time to drink beer and work on his art because his wife paid the rent in their subsidized flat and because she was too kind to leave him. I didn't think he was faithful to her. He did not seem like the faithful kind. The exhibit at Kayseri, I thought, was a spread of Paul's indiscretion.

And I admired him for it.

I admired the way he had cobbled together these scraps of bone and wax and tape recordings of himself talking on the telephone. He had made molds from scrap wood and old tires and poured his forms with hand-mixed concrete. The installation had been set up in the long foyer of the university's art building and during the exhibition Paul spent a good deal of his time outside in the patches of the last, dirty, ice-packed snow, smoking and pacing. I thought the curve of rusted wire remarkable the way he had threaded it through an empty 5-liter tin for olive oil, as was the sound of his voice blinking on and off from inside the cassette player, wrapped in paper. I didn't talk to him much. I mean, I said, *Hello*, and I stayed as long as was reasonable, and then I had some tea at the canteen and got on the bus back to the hotel in the village.

I didn't feel like I knew a whole lot about art or what was going on in the world of installation, but I was very sure these pieces did not come from someone who was contented.

What stunned me most was his shame in it, how he didn't want to watch us watching his honey drip, hear us hearing his loop play. *Come inside*, I had wanted to say to him when I'd catch the half moon of his head in one of the windows, *It's perfectly okay*. He stayed outside, though, the smoke curling through the half frozen air.

•

We did go to the mountain, a few days later. I convinced Yasemin to come along, and I packed us all a lunch and dry socks. We caught a shared taxi from Kayseri and bounced along in the backmost seat of the minibus as it traversed the mountain road. Twice, we stopped to pick up more passengers, and twice we all piled out and arranged ourselves in groups of men and women, and then piled back in so that no man and woman shared a bench.

When we reached the ski village at Mount Erciyes, the chairlift was zinging up into a fog. Though April was just around the corner, there was still plenty of snow, though it had lost its winter fluff. We hadn't planned on skiing, or snowshoeing, or even sledding, but Paul had the idea that we should climb higher. We decided that none of us wanted to pay the full ticket price, so Paul and I watched as Yasemin worked on the lift operator. A few pieces of her hair had come loose from her headscarf, and her skin looked almost opalescent. She finally convinced him to let us go up for one fare if we could fit three people in the double chair.

We rode to the top of the first crests, me in the middle. Yasemin and I pulled our scarves down tighter on our heads; Paul adjusted his hat. The snow stung against my cheeks, and Paul's thigh stung against mine.

I trusted him—the day he'd left the hotel and Yasemin finished my curtains, he said he was meeting with a friend who would be going to Istanbul, and I gave him a letter to hand off. I addressed it to Julian and sealed it and dug out a few lira for postage. Inside, I wrote, *I really am okay. I really do love you. I really am coming back. Love, Laura,* in block letters on an otherwise blank sheet of paper, and I made him promise that he wouldn't open the envelope and that he must impress upon his friend not to mail it until he reached Istanbul proper—it's a big city, twice the size of New York, so I thought the postmark would be safe enough. I didn't want Julian showing up in Göreme. It was better if he thought I was on the move, back to a place with a major airport. I could have easily logged in at any of the Internet shops in Anatolia and sent the same message, but I thought that if I were on the other side of it, I'd want something that had been touched. Paul didn't ask me anything about not including a return address, or who might live on Jackson Street, in Seattle.

"I will explain it to my friend," he said.

"Thank you," I said.

"My pleasure," he said.

As the chairlift neared the turn where it would head back down, we piled off onto the ramp and slid into the drifts. We'd seen a few spring skiers here and there, but I think none of us were really sure what to do once we'd gotten up there. We started hiking toward a clump of trees, where we sat down to rest and watch the light snow that had begun to fall. It occurred to me that I was really not wearing the right shoes.

"What do you think," said Paul, "is it true that no two snowflakes are alike?"

"It is simply fact," said Yasemin. Her voice was soft.

Paul tipped his head toward hers as if he expected her to elaborate, but she didn't.

From there we decided we would make our way down the hill. I had my small pack, and Yasemin had another. Paul was empty-handed, and he offered to take both our bags. I kept mine. Yasemin kept hers, too.

This trip was like many things in Turkey; we would do things for the sheer sake of it—it was like counting bees or organizing kinds of sand: distracting, entertaining sometimes, and almost wholly pointless. We just keep walking, pointing our bodies *down*, which is hardly even a direction.

The snow was picking up, and it was like egg whites being beaten into meringue, the clear air swirling into thick. I wondered how much time the geographer Strabo might have really spent on the slopes. The going would have been slower and colder then, without chairlifts and advances in outerwear.

There were a few more hours before the light would fail, but partway down the hill, Yasemin pointed out that the lift had stopped even intermittent operation. We'd been keeping close to the base of the lift as a guide. When I looked up, the empty chairs swung like shoes thrown over low power lines.

I think we all noticed how quiet it had become. The snow was coming down harder and my feet were getting cold. I felt a little nervous. I had grown up in rural Washington state in a drafty house with wood heat, and so I had learned to fear cold in winter just as fire in summer.

For a moment, I prayed for my practical husband. He would not have let me go out without proper boots; he would have a flashlight and a flare.

That's when Paul stepped in between Yasemin and me and took us each by the hand.

"Ladies?" he said.

I liked holding Paul's hand, even through gloves.

"Do you rescue us?" Yasemin asked him.

"No," he said, "I just want to hold onto something." He laughed.

Our linked hands made the going even slower, but there were several times each of us nearly fell, and the others kept us upright. It seemed forever before we saw the lights at the base of the ski hill, and the cold only grew, but when we finally made it, we got excited and tossed snowballs at Paul. The lodge had closed, so he went off to check the other teahouse.

As Yasemin and I waited for Paul to come back, I saw how her already pink cheeks had turned red in the cold. We laughed at how we must look, with our wet pants and frozen fingers, loitering in the failing light, our heads and shoulders dotted with snowflakes.

I think I was bold with fear when I said to Yasemin that I really enjoyed being with Paul, who was coming back toward us, and then I felt a stab. I was wrong to admit it.

When I was nine, my mother hoisted me into the chair at the jewelry counter of the Rexall in town, and I waited for the clerk to nip each ear with steel—it wasn't the pain but the anticipation that made me feel funny, that made me nearly fall from the high stool; and once it was done, I felt a rush of adrenalin and terror, just like I did now.

"I know," Yasemin said. "I know, *canim*." I liked that she used this endearment, *my dear*, with me.

Of course she knew, but I was relieved anyway. The snow fell around us and from a certain angle it looked like vertical sheets, like a white flag.

We learned from Paul we had missed the final transport off the slopes—it had left early, and full, as the snow intensified. Even when we were highest, I certainly hadn't been able to make out any of the surrounding seas that Strabo had written about. Perhaps it's easy to invent a few details—a crest here, an ocean there—when you imagine no one will retrace your steps.

The café on the main road was open, and we went there and drank tea. I passed out the dry socks, and we had our sandwiches. There were only a few other people inside the café, but Yasemin asked around anyway; none of them planned to head down the mountain.

We sat close in a circular booth, with me in the middle. Under the table, I put my cold sock foot on top of Paul's and aligned our toes. I kept my hands up and in plain view.

After the first cups were finished, we took more tea and Paul sorted his change on the table. He put on his shoes and plugged the small jukebox. When he came back to the booth, he wiggled his foot loose from his boot and placed it on top of mine.

When we found hope of nothing else, Yasemin rewrapped her scarf and went out to the road to hitchhike. We watched her from the window, the snow sifting around her like confectioner's sugar—a pious bride atop our cake Erciyes.

Alone with Paul, I wished I had something to say. I tried to compliment him on his show, but he didn't want to talk about it. We ordered more tea. We peeked out the window at Yasemin. He was married, but he kept his toes stacked on my toes. I was married, but I kept my ring under the mattress at the hotel. I had already thought of selling it at one of the gold markets.

When a box truck finally stopped, we crammed our feet into our shoes and ran out to meet Yasemin as she begged the driver to take us back to town. She pretended that she did not really know us. She had gone out alone because we all understood that someone who would stop for a local, covered woman in a snowstorm might not stop for two Americans with their laces untied. She told the driver she had come up to Erciyes on a sick call, and that she must get back to her husband in town. She said she did not know so much about these *yabancı*, foreigners, and what we were doing, but she knew we had nowhere to go.

In the end, Paul sat up in front, and Yasemin and I rode down in the back. She said the driver told her that he would have rather put the Americans in the back, but he was concerned how it would look driving into Kayseri at night with a woman on his passenger side. She agreed.

I had ridden in the back of many trucks, but never like this. It was a vehicle made for hauling meat, and it was filled with hooks and an undercurrent of carrion. Yasemin and I sat against the wheel well, leaning into each other for heat.

"You have to be very careful," Yasemin said. She sounded angry.

I thought she meant taking on Erciyes and forcing her to hitchhike.

"I'm sorry," I said. "I didn't know it would snow so much."

"No, Laura, not the snow. Not the *kar.*" Yasemin frowned. She must have been thinking about it while she was flagging the truck, while she convinced him to take three. "You have to be careful with the men here," she said. "And you. You need to be careful with you."

"I'm sorry," I said again. I knew then just how much she saw, about everything.

The truck groaned, the hooks rattled above us. It was cold.

I wondered about the secrets Yasemin might have of her own.

After the meat truck dropped us off in Kayseri, Paul walked us most of the way back to the bus station, and he tried to tell us the driver's story, but neither of us were interested. I had gotten something in my right eye, a piece of straw or animal hair, I wasn't sure, and the entire surface was irritated and weeping.

When he left us, a few yards from the bus station, in the dark, I was surprised at how the day had turned. I had hoped he would come back to the village, rent a room at the hotel, sit with Yasemin and me, and finish a few bottles of local wine and get warm with us.

I would have settled even for having him touch my frozen hair here in the dark. When we did return to the hotel, I went straight to my place. The light was so low that even the orange curtains looked dull.

I think that when I was with Paul, I didn't feel so stupid for failing to return to the US. We had talked only vaguely about how we'd both been surprised to find ourselves jammed in between the things that had become our life, but there was understanding.

Mostly, Julian had happened to me. Anne had happened to us. I had my work and my daughter and my husband. I had my parents, whom I didn't see much, on the other side of the state. I could visit them more; I could push on them some to visit me. I regretted not keeping them closer.

My parents had worked very hard in our little rural town. Yet, my two brothers and I had left, as early as we could. I wondered if my folks thought this was a success or a failure.

I, in particular, had been driven; always sure I would leave, even though Seattle wasn't really that far. The piece of me I thought of as still being kept by Daniel was the piece of the place I couldn't let go.

A homescape.

Our shared geography.

The smell of hay and raspberry bushes—the idyllic things in country life, and also the violence. Fire. Mercy killings of animals.

Now I could close my eyes and see the imprint of mosques, the minaret reaching for sky, the rough edges of the stone walls, and I felt close to the land again.

Then, it was as clear as a clean window, as the *imam's* voice at dawn, that I would not be returning to America before the summer came.

I thought of what I had said about Paul to Yasemin and what she had said to me. I hoped she was not too angry. Just a heady mistake, from cold, from being scared in the deep snow with only tennis shoes and a scarf from the tourist markets.

In my bed, curled in the quilts, I did not wish for him. I wished for Anne, and Julian, almost, because he'd helped me make her.

•

The days sped up after our trip to Erciyes, and Yasemin and I both opened up some. One day, after hours of working, she turned her head to the side and said, "Yeah, you live in the village now, we will gossip."

Did I look scared?

In those days I learned she had been raised here. She described her parents as stern but loving, but the more she told me, the more I imagined them like a ball of yarn, the line of their lives wrapped around some invisible center, a center that, if you unrolled the whole mass, turned out to not be there at all. Therefore do not pick at the knots. Therefore hold your end of the string.

I knew that feeling.

Pull.

I mean that I felt that same sense of being tangled around dead air or a barren peach, around something that is empty. Sometimes the bright chips in the kaleidoscope are just that—little bits of nothing. Sometimes there is no picture at all.

Silver shoes, a rusty car. Growing up in dirt and heat and having chores. A husband and a daughter.

I thought maybe the outcome was the same, as in unknown.

When she described her childhood, I thought of Anne, my girl, and wondered if she would remember being young the same way, with her own tiny world, a bubble of light against the tall gray adults. In other ways they were not the same.

It wasn't that I didn't ache for Anastasia. It was impossible not to. She came from me. She lived inside of me. I loved her more than I could even articulate. And that's also how I could stand to be away from her, I think. I did love her, and I thought, when I tried to rationalize, that a *good* mother would take time for herself. A *good* mother would make sure she wasn't missing a few marbles, and I was trying. But that wasn't exactly it. She was only seven, but I trusted her. I trusted her in a way I didn't trust my own mother, Julian, or longtime friends, or Daniel. I trusted that she was okay without me. I still felt as though I barely knew Yasemin, but she was the only person—her strange, heavy eyebrows, her deep, heavy voice—who even came close to matching how I felt for Anne. Paul was something different.

Yasemin had grown up knowing how to roll out flat breads, to plant gardens, to watch sheep. She learned English when she was in college—she'd won a scholarship and studied chemistry at a university in Ankara, the capital.

One day in the kitchen she told me how Ankara was a world like nothing she'd ever seen. I had read in the guidebook that it had grown from a town of three thousand to a city of four million in less than eighty years, and Yasemin said it gleamed with newness in this old place, she said, *gleamed.* We looked up the word just to be sure.

She studied very hard, earning high marks and the respect of her professors; she loved chemistry.

The predictable way molecules changed each other.

The pretty rows of clean glassware and the long, black lab tables.

And a boy with green eyes.

Like at many of the private schools, her classes at the university were in English, so she'd spent a year at the preparatory school, but it wasn't until she got to her actual chemistry lessons that the language became real. *Nickel, calcium, boron,* she said. Like an incantation. The names on the periodic table and the *periyodik tablo* were certainly spelled different, but many of the sounds were close, and it was still all foreign to her. She learned *lithium*—one of the few elements in the earliest universe—is soft and burns crimson.

And, Yasemin went out with a bare head for the first time since she'd begun bleeding, which was when her mother tucked her hair up in a scarf, as was tradition in the village, and showed her how to knot it so it would stay put through the day.

In Ankara, Yasemin let the air onto her neck; her black hair turned copper in the sun.

When the boy with the green eyes watched her, she watched him back.

"It was my first love affair," she told me. "And when we finished the first year, it ended."

When she told me this, it was on a day we were making cheese. She told me the story of how cheese had come to be: a handsome Arab crossing the desert carried milk with him, using the sheep's stomach as a container. When he opened the belly, he saw it had separated, and when he tasted what was left of his milk, because he was hungry, he was delighted.

We made it the same way—swapping the guts for a steel pan—with only milk and rennet. Sometimes Yasemin added salt, but not too much when she was expecting more Western tourists.

"Sodium," she whispered, "bad for them."

And so she also told me, after that first emerald boy, each year she had a new lover, and by the end of final exams, he was gone. She craved the sweat of sex, the way one smelled like newly cut grass, the pretty fingers of another who ought to have been studying music, but by the time spring gave way to the unforgiving heat of summer, she wanted her body back, and she left them, and she continued reciting the table: *uranium, iron, antimony.* Ninety-two naturally occurring elements.

When Yasemin graduated, she returned to the village. She had thought of going on to do an advanced degree, but her father was aging quickly, and her mother wanted her home. She was not the perfect Muslim girl, but she was kind, and she loved her family.

"In America women still make these kinds of sacrifices too," I said to her. "You choose your people or your profession."

"Tell me," she said, "how come the Arab boy's milk did not simply rot?"

I looked at her, blankly.

"I wanted to choose both," she said. "I think you can do this, a little bit, in America?"

"*Anliyorum,*" I said. *I understand.* My first verb.

"Good," she said.

The next day, we stood on the roof terrace beating carpets. Yasemin explained that she preferred to clean the carpets in winter. She said the best way was in the first skiffs of dry snow, dumping the carpets face down on the crystals and stomping out the dirt—Anatolian dry cleaning. However, the dregs of March were too wet, and the carpets would not wait.

Weaving was popular in this central, inland region, and Yasemin had both antique and family pieces, and the average practice pieces that she got from a shop a few streets up. The shop was laden with carpets and travelers, and in the front they employed covered girls to sit on the porch and thread cheap wool through oversized looms all day, just for looks. The girls made more of these basic carpets than the shop could ever hope to sell, and Yasemin bought them for the cost of materials and piled them in her guest rooms, so we always had something to clean. I tried once to explain to her about using a vacuum cleaner. She had heard of it and one of her friends had had one in Ankara. She was not impressed.

I wasn't expecting it, but there, on her roof, as we thrashed at the carpets as surely as the cobbler had hammered his shoes, she told me the rest.

When Yasemin, after graduating with honors, returned to her hometown, she felt it was normal for her, come fall, though she would not be back at school, to look for someone new.

She was living under her father's roof again, and while her parents lamented that she had lost some of her piety—going around with her bare head like that—they were not fundamentalists and were pleased to have her home. Even as she returned to the gardens, to the kitchen, and the cycle of daily chores, she missed the pinch of goggles on her nose and the obscene whiteness of her lab coat; but she was content enough, squeezing lemon into soda for her baking. She knew what made it fizz.

She had thought of staying in Ankara and looking for a job, but she really had missed the village, her parents, the smell of rock.

I thought of Daniel, our childhood. I thought how it had been too many days since I'd written my daughter.

In early September, one of their neighbors came for dinner, and Yasemin saw a flash in her head, the color-blocked arrangement of the squares of the table, the names returning to her tongue—*neon, nitrogen, cobalt*—and she looked closely at this guest, who she saw was certainly older than her, though substantially younger than her father, with skin the color of a walnut hull and a wad of curly hair, which he wore just a few centimeters too long for the conservative styles of the village.

Her parents, then, were trying to arrange a marriage with the son of another farming family, and she wanted none of it.

Onur was already married, but Yasemin knew she could have him.

She sighed and looked at me. "Sometimes we can see the future," she said.

And she could see him, easily, without his dusty clothes, skin bronzed and slick, but even so, the crystal was clouded.

I nodded at her. It was a warm day. We finished our pounding, hung the rugs over the courtyard railing, and went in to make tea.

She told it as an easy, predictable seduction. A hand brushed, an elbow touched. Then meeting behind the chicken coop or in his stable of donkeys, the infrequency and the secrecy pushing her toward him, the crack of jealousy when she heard his wife, Fatma, was newly pregnant.

Sulfur, aluminum, arsenic.

That November, Yasemin didn't notice the new cold; again she could feel the heat of the fall, its fire colors.

I remember looking at my hands, how the skin was peeling off my fingers from Yasemin's dishwater. "If it doesn't hurt, it's not hot," she would always say to me and pour scalding water from her kettle into my pan.

In late October, she went to see Onur. They had an hour arranged, she said, and they pushed it to an hour and a half.

She pushed it.

His wife had walked to the other side of the village to deliver something to her mother, and the early snows had begun again. Yasemin remembered how clearly Onur said that his wife enjoyed walking but would expect him to pick her up because of the weather, and he was late. Yasemin ducked out the back door as he jogged to the car.

Even though she didn't seem quite close enough, she heard the tires, and she heard a *thump*, the sound of beating a drum with a loose head or the dropping of a heavy load.

Fatma's body across the back hatch.

Blood on the new snow.

Yasemin ran down the road and after the car, not more than twenty yards, slipping and falling the entire way, and she saw, with her eye trained for the observation of science, exactly what had happened: having taken a sharp corner too fast, Onur slid into a 180-degree turn and sideswiped Fatma, catching her against the back bumper, and now she was slumped against the car, bent wrong.

Onur saw Yasemin come around the turn, and he looked straight at her, she told me. *Go*, he called to her, helpless with his scarlet bride.

And she did. She ran.

•

I woke from a dream about Anne that I couldn't remember. I knew there was fire. I thought maybe she was in the caves with us, her light body perched on the back of a boar.

In the dream, she had been the other daughter, the one that had been of Daniel and me. I knew because of the green eyes staring out. It was not yet morning and my single bed seemed to have become smaller overnight, like lying on a plank, scared of the drop, me another of those mutinous sailors who can't swim.

I had gone deep enough into the hole of doubt to stop looking for handholds.

I put on the old wrapper Yasemin had given me and opened my door into the lower courtyard. The air was still cruel at night, but I stepped out of my room anyway.

What was I thinking of then?

I did feel the pull of her, but when I started to think of returning, I got slack.

I had never believed in the pure biology of motherhood—clocks and so forth—and even when she was born, the instinct to push my breast to her screaming mouth was not so different, I thought, than the instinct to smash my hand against the snooze of an alarm clock: just make the noise stop. But maybe I didn't mean that.

Now I had a perfect quiet.

When she was first born, I had always listened so hard for Anne's shriek—the one she'd grown out of quickly, the voice she had before she could control any of her sounds, just the wail of raw shock at her new tertian world and the experience of need for the first time—I could hear all the other sounds that weren't there, hushed voices and padded footsteps, each rustle or muffled clunk the simple pattern of my own blood.

•

I had two sets of sheets for my bed at Yasemin's place. White cotton printed with blue roses, and white cotton printed with yellow roses. She made sure I put them in the wash at least twice a week.

My soiled laundry.

Our red, raw hands.

Off the wash line, I wrapped myself in the clean cloth, a cocoon, and I waited patiently for the transformation.

I waited for Julian, too.

I considered his intelligence, the people he knew, that matter cannot be created nor disappear. *He could find me*, I whispered to myself, not sure if it was hope or fear. *He said he would find me*, but I also remembered I had asked him not to. And he could be going on alone; one stone in the bottom of a riverbed that doesn't much care if another tumbles away.

I kept going for long walks. Yasemin sketched me rough maps, and I picked along the rocks, skirting the new-tilled fields in the many small, sudden valleys. I visited the old pre-Islam churches and trekked to the underground cities with their pissy smell of wood smoke, but it was in the open air where I was happiest, surprised every time by the geology, the columns shaped like mushrooms or a man's sex, the gentle erosion on the hillsides exposing pink and sand. Whenever I heard the call to prayer, I stopped. Though Mecca was to the east, I turned west, toward where I knew my family was, to what had until now been my home.

I avoided the tourists, of which there were many, just as dazed as having stepped off the bus and into a children's picture book as I had been. To Yasemin's guests, I was courteous but not over-friendly. I was at their disposal to run out for cigarettes or recommend a spot for lunch. I didn't learn their names, ask about their holidays or origins, just stripped their beds and rinsed their smells away, erased their footprints from the carpet.

I started to think that maybe it was time to move on. I thought of Yasemin's story of her lover and his wife often. I wondered if she had loved him, and I wondered if it mattered. Sometimes I sat down at the small table in my room and I thought of writing Julian a real letter, but I couldn't. There was nothing I knew to say to him. Finally, I did send Anne some more postcards. I wrote out a few things, carefully, and in clean script. *I love you, I miss you, I'll come home when I can.* I decided to put them in envelopes to hide what I'd written, stamped, and then asked Paul to drop them in a mailbox the next time he or a friend was in Istanbul or Ankara, like I had done with the first note to Julian.

One day Yasemin called from the side door of the kitchen to where I was on the lowest terrace. She was holding a pot of lentils, and with sweat beading off her face, she said, "Yeah, you know Onur? My lover?"

"Yeah," I said.

"He owns that carpet shop."

"The one down the street?" I asked.

"*Evet.*" *Yes.* "You know we had some trouble, but we still deal." She looked at me for a moment and then turned, her back sloped a little with the weight of the food, her elbows pointed. The door slammed behind her.

Okay, I thought. *Go call. Go make phone calls. Just use the credit card.*

I poked my head into the kitchen, where she was sweating as heavily as the lentil pot, and asked Yasemin if she needed any help, but she waved me away.

It would be late at night in America, but I walked to the payphone booth anyway. It was Friday, my almost day off.

April had finally come and with it the real spring, and all around me were tiny blooms.

I hesitated, not sure which number to dial first, but once the tip of my finger depressed the first digit, it was easy to dial the rest. I left a long message on Julian's cell phone—*Listen, I know I'm asking a lot of you. I know it. I'm just trying to figure something out. I'm staying and working at a little hotel. It's called* Bahçe Evi, *it means* Garden House. *I don't think there's a website. There's a phone but I don't know the number. I'll get the number.* I told him I was okay, I told him I understood if he wanted a divorce, though I did not really want a divorce. I told him I was *sorry, sorry, sorry, sorry,* and I could understand if he didn't understand. I promised to check my email. I told him, *Thank you. Thank you for our daughter, and thank you for being patient, however much you have left.*

Raised in another era, I knew my mother would jolt awake at the sound of the telephone. She came from a time when people had manners about phone calls—even we, as children, had to ask permission to use the phone—and the sound of the ringer through the dark usually meant trouble.

"Hi," I said. "It's only me."

"Laura," she said. "Dear Lord. Are you in the airport? Please."

"No, Mom. I'm not. How are you?"

She let me change the subject. We talked for some time, the charges ticking by on the credit card. I wondered what Julian would think when he saw the bill. She gave me the update on her and my father, nothing much, and said my brothers were well. Tentatively, I told her about the town I was in, about Yasemin. I told her how much I missed Anastasia. I knew what she was thinking, that I could fix that kind of hurt anytime by going home, but she didn't say it.

"I'll tell your father you're doing just fine," she said.

"Thanks," I said.

After we hung up, I left messages for Richard and for Michael, and tried Julian again, just in case.

And then, because I was there and the light in the phone booth was already shining, I tried Daniel's old home number, the one I'd dialed so many times before late at night, which I knew by heart. But, like every time, after four rings, the answering machine—same message as always on the scratchy tape—picked up, Daniel's father's voice sounding through the dark, empty rooms, while I stood in broad daylight.

CHAPTER THREE

Spring for me had always held a randy feeling of discontent. I was never able to fully describe it. The closest I could ever come up with was the feeling of that kind of sex that people must wait to have—maybe they need the perfect combination of beer and sunshine, the right coworker on the right business trip.

When I was a child, spring would come fast. One day I'd be pulling up my thick cotton tights, layering a sweater over my dress, and tromping around in boots, and then it seemed in only moments the weather would break, and I would be on immediately to galoshes caked with thick, just-melted mud. From there it was only a few more breaths until the ground gave way to the earlies, rows of lavender crocus and shimmering daffodils peeking through the garden.

As an adult, one thing I had liked about living on the other side of Washington in Seattle's temperate climate was that the spring was never as violent as in other places, like the place of my childhood. Unlike the east, the western part of the state stays green year round, and while the sky is petulant, spitting little bursts of misty rain, at another angle the long gray days look silver or pewter. I liked the way the clouds softened the edges of the skyline, and I liked how the fog made everything twinkle.

Talking to Yasemin had pushed me, but I think it might have really been the weather that made me walk to the phone booth I passed almost every day, the weather that made me step across the space from the sidewalk onto the white tile with the feeling of something about to burst—an ice dam, a bulb's root, a blister when it's finally out of winter boots.

When I got back to Yasemin's, I felt like I'd been on a bender and was just coming out of it, flush with indulgence. She was still in the kitchen.

"What's the phone number here?" I asked.

"On the phone. I wrote it on the phone," she said. The lentils had transformed into a rapidly bubbling soup.

Julian, I'm sure, thought it was something about responsibility. He had a tendency to defer to the trappings of adult life as if there were no other choice. As if it were something like getting past the age of being able to order off the children's menu, and simply accepting he'd never get to eat a peanut butter and jelly sandwich in a restaurant again. I figured there were a couple ways to handle it, like to lie about one's age, lie about the recipient (*Oh, it's for my daughter—she's at home*), or point to the senior menu. Finally, it helped sometimes to beg. All of these had worked for me. Julian, though, didn't think like that. And he certainly didn't think that if he were able to talk the server into it, that he should then just go ahead and ask for the crusts cut off too.

There was a way he spoke sometimes—I wished I had gotten to hear his voice, and I wished he would have answered, so he could put Anne on the line—a way he styled himself as being in control. When I first met him, I'd liked that. His hands were sure on me, and his touch had the feel of practice, like someone who'd learned to French braid their own hair behind their head or throw a pot. He was a smart man, but frustrating sometimes; typical in that he could use his work as an excuse for anything—for being irritable, for getting off the phone quickly, for coming home late.

Sometimes I felt like that was all I was doing—coming home late.

He never had lipstick on his collar or smelled like a bar, and right now neither did I.

When I married him, I thought my vows would be what tethered me to him. And then when Anne was born, I thought it would be her.

I found where Yasemin had taped the digits for the line, where the receiver met the cradle, and copied them carefully, adding the country code, 90, so I wouldn't forget to tell him, and put the scrap of paper in my pocket.

"We have people," said Yasemin when I circled back to the kitchen. "I met them at the bus stop."

"Good," I said.

"I hope they eat," she said, stirring the soup.

Our guests were a gift; a group of four retired couples traveling together, who were very, very tired. Checking them in, I chatted with them some about the distance they had come, all the way from Akron, Ohio, and what they planned to do. I suggested an easy hike.

We joined them in the dining room, where they were visibly pleased that everything was right there, warm food, soft light, a local to soothe them, me a bridge between countries.

"How do you say *thank you* in Turkish?" one of the women asked me.

"*Teşekkürler*," I said. "It's a hard one. *Teşekkürler ederim*, if you want to be a little more formal. Also, everyone understands *thank you*, but Turks, they will be happy if you try, even if you get it really, really wrong."

"Tesh shek you," she said.

"Good," I said. "Very close."

Yasemin smiled at me and I smiled back. We both knew my Turkish was so horrible I should not be giving anyone advice.

That night, after the dishes were clean, I went back to the phone booth and dialed Julian. It would be morning now.

Julian's voice was unsure as he answered. I wondered if he saw the flash of many digits across the caller ID—perhaps he knew it was me, or he dreaded it.

"It's Laura," I said. My name felt funny on my tongue.

"Laura." I could hear the catch in his voice.

"Hi." I watched the meter tick.

"I got your message," he said.

"Right," I said. I read him the phone number.

"We can get you a ticket today," he said. "You can be home by tomorrow."

I wanted to tell him that it was already evening and tomorrow would come fast.

"How is Anne?" I asked. My tongue felt strange around her name as well.

"She's better," he said. "She wants to know why you haven't called her."

"Can I talk to her?" I said this before I was sure if it was a good idea. How would I feel to hear her voice?

"No," he said. "I mean, she's not here. She's at your mother's. It's difficult for me, you know, to live like this. If you want a divorce, Laura, just say so. Don't leave us waiting."

"I said I didn't. I said it was up to you."

I heard him sigh. The meter kept ticking.

I imagined him in his pressed shirt, on the hall phone, twirling his key ring around his index finger the way he did when he was on his way to somewhere else. I imagined flying backward in time to meet him. I imagined the smell of our house and of Anne's hair.

"What about school, if she's at my parents'?"

"They have a school there," he said. "You know that."

"A shitty school," I said. "I just talked to Mom yesterday. She didn't say Anne was with her."

"I thought I should tell you," he said.

There was some silence, and then static.

"I'm going to go now," I said, and I put the phone back into its cradle, lifted it again and dialed my mother. I knew I was a hypocrite to be so angry, and I imagined what Julian might say.

What did you expect?

Maybe my heart had never been quite full for him.

And, maybe his had never been quite full for me.

•

The next day, Yasemin came to me with a gift. Sometimes I would think that I could never possibly be more grateful toward her, and then she would surprise me again.

I wondered if any of her lovers had shown her these same kindnesses.

When she handed me the bag, I recognized it from the market—simple brown paper with the price of potatoes scrawled on one side. She'd made a bow out of scrap from a sewing project.

"Thank you for all your helping," she said.

I was surprised by the weight, and inside, I found a mobile phone. It was large and clunky, screen a dead black. It must have been my week for telecommunications. Of modernity in an old place.

"This is too expensive," I said.

"No," she said. "This is only the phone. You have to purchase the credits if you want to talk or send a message. I only bought a few credits to start with so I could open your number."

This from a woman who didn't own a vacuum.

Really, I only knew her and Paul, but I knew Paul had a mobile. Everyone had a mobile. I had even seen a television commercial featuring boys working as sheepherders—and it wasn't a joke, as sheep-, goat-, and cow-herding were alive and well as a profession— encouraging families to make sure their phone always had credits so young shepherds could text their *baba* if a lamb went missing.

Normally, if I could say I *liked* electronics, I liked them small—I liked them not to intrude. For years, before I married, I'd owned the same television, a fourteen-inch black and white one that once I'd painted pink with tempura and shellacked over. It was ridiculous, but I could keep it in the closet where it wouldn't get in the way. People raised in the country are like this, and we have different ideas about what is okay and what is not.

I liked the heft of the mobile phone, though. I liked the possibility. I thought maybe I was ready to be a little more connected. The conversation with Julian had not gone well, but maybe I was only out of practice.

I powered the phone on. Yasemin had programmed her number in, and she'd changed the language settings to English.

"Thank you," I told her. I dialed her number and let it ring once, just to test, then hung up so I wouldn't waste my credits. Her phone beeped.

"Really," I said. "It's too much."

"Laura. Someone dropped this phone at the carpet shop, and Onur said it has been more than one week. That is his rule, he says."

"Okay." I said. "Thank you."

For the rest of the day, I kept the phone in my pocket. When we baked bread, it pressed into my hip as I leaned against the counter to knead. When I scrubbed the floor after, the heavy plastic of it made my loose pants sag toward the floor on one side, as I picked at the bits of dough smeared across the tiles.

I wondered if Yasemin meant anything by such a gift. One of the many reasons that I liked her was because she was thoughtful—not thoughtful in the nice way, thoughtful in the contemplative way.

Did she think this was another way for me to ring someone across the ocean?

Did she think a phone might be the first in the many trappings that could keep me in the country?

Did she know my first thought was that I would have a more reliable way for Paul to contact me?

When she said we should break before we took our dinner and served our guests, I went directly to my room and keyed in Paul's digits off the scrap of paper I kept folded between the pages of my travel guide.

I sent him a text. This was my first mobile phone, but I did know that in Turkey, text was the preferred way to communicate.

HELLO. THIS IS LAURA. NOW YOU HAVE MY NUMBER.

The electronic sound—like glass breaking—as he replied startled and thrilled me.

HEY!! DO YOU WANT TO GO TO ANKARA THIS WEEKEND? I HAVE FRIENDS THERE.

It was Tuesday, and so I didn't respond. I would have to ask Yasemin for time off. And I would have to think about it.

With the change in seasons, business had picked up some. Yasemin had mentioned that she might be able to start paying me, and anticipating some money of my own gave me the same feel as stepping off of the plane had, the same thrill as the phone: drudge turned to hope. I was getting down to my last few bills.

After the group from Akron left, we had some more Americans and an Austrian couple. We took our meals with guests, only if they invited us. Sometimes, they would want to get recommendations from Yasemin on attractions, sometimes they would be caught in the spin of feeling too far from home and would want to be left alone.

The foreign borders at Yasemin's hotel loved her meals. I know she got tired of the same rounds of hearty, starch-heavy village food, but I didn't. Lentil soup, bready meatballs, salads of tomato and pepper chopped with fine parsley and lemon.

I had the idea of purchasing some bottled water and reusing the bottles at our table—I told Yasemin that Americans, at least, generally believed the taps in other countries to be unsafe, and this had gone over well with both her and our North American travelers.

That night, our six guests helped themselves generously from the table. One of the Americans—her name was Elisa, and she was thin in the way well-kept women are sometimes, with wispy blond-gray hair and a scarf I recognized from one of the shops wrapped around her neck—asked if there might be some wine for purchase.

Yasemin said, "Of course," and cocked her head at me.

I went to the small pantry we had off the kitchen and grabbed one of our wine bottles. We had only one kind: local stuff, decent but not fancy.

I uncorked the bottle and brought glasses to the table.

It was hard not to think of my husband. I'd spent more nights than I really wanted to admit like this, in Seattle, heading for the pantry for wine.

Sometimes we'd have guests who would have already gone home, and sometimes we would have been on our own all evening, but either way found me sitting on the porch in the dark or near-dark, sneaking a cigarette and making my way through the last bottle, while Julian worked on his laptop in the office.

Sometimes he would come outside and stare at me for a minute, and I would stare back at him. I wanted to talk to him, but I couldn't make the words come out, I didn't know what to say to him. I was as mute as the cork, my mouth woody.

I remembered now that even if I couldn't find space in my heart for Julian, that I had before. When I met him, I hadn't known what to do with him at first—he was so different from anyone else I knew—but once I got used to him, his halo of curls and the way he smelled like mowing the lawn, green and gasoline, I had fallen for him. I had fallen for the idea of a permanent pairing very, very hard and we married quickly, at the courthouse, in spring. It was the first working day after the three-day waiting period. I had a silver band with moons and stars on it that we'd gotten from a trinkety kind of jeweler, and it cost just under fifteen dollars. I helped him pick it out and we laughed about it. If the rule was two month's salary, since he was between jobs just then, it was a real splurge. Later, we got him one very similar.

We always talked about upgrading to something different, but we didn't until the finishing wore off and

I got a rash from the nickel. I'd gone around with my finger bare for a year before he surprised me with the simple gold band stashed in my room now. Our anniversary was coming up.

At Yasemin's table, I started pouring the wine, beginning with the woman Elise and then her husband, and finally their two friends. She gestured that the Austrians should get a pour as well, and Yasemin and I.

Yasemin, I knew, took only a splash. I had learned that Turkish Muslims are generally not as rigorous about alcohol as some others, but the rules were still different for women than men, especially in public. While I didn't agree with the different gender rules, I liked the temperate religion.

I still felt the call to prayer as I had in Istanbul, sometimes deeply.

I'd still never actually gone to a mosque during prayer, but for me, raised agnostic and turned atheist, the gentle, sacred touch on daily life felt kind and real. Yasemin had told me in the east of the country, people were much stricter, and girls left school at twelve to be apprenticed in the home to learn domesticity. Yet, even just a few hundred miles west, even in our village, there were plenty of women who walked bareheaded and had a cocktail now and again.

"You might want to get another bottle," Elise said. "Eight glasses is a few too many for just one." She smiled at me.

"In *Türkçe*," Yasemin said, "we say *şerife* before we drink and *afiyet olsun* before we eat."

"Sort of like *cheers* and *bon appétit*," I said.

"Cheers!" said Elise.

"*Proust!*" said the Austrian man.

Our glasses clinked.

The meal went well. There were compliments for Yasemin and me, and a third bottle of wine was opened. Yasemin gave me a look when I topped off my glass, but when she saw my face turn at being chastised, her look softened, and I tipped in another glug.

We moved to dessert, a plate of fruit. In the traditional way, Yasemin peeled the oranges, apples, and bananas for everyone and passed pieces around the table. I liked to watch her skin the fruit with her quick knife. I liked how easily she cored, how easily she stripped the rinds.

It was like a lesson in efficiency, a lesson in getting straight to the heart.

We opened the fourth bottle. The Austrians were not rowdy, but they'd started speaking loudly, switching often between English and German, and when the plates were put away, they asked if they could smoke, and we all nodded

"*Tabi, tabi,*" said Yasemin. *Of course.*

I also pulled a cigarette from a pack, and Elise asked if she might have one.

"I've been quit for years," she said and winked in the sly, endearing way of older women.

I lit it for her and heard the singe of paper, the tobacco light.

"You know," she said, "you look familiar."

I dropped my lighter on the floor and bent to pick it up, the mobile phone pinching my thigh.

"Really?" I said.

"You do," she said.

Yasemin was eyeing us. The room had gone wispy, the curls from cigarettes pooling above our heads. The Austrian man blew smoke rings; his wife tried but her smoke came out in a laugh.

"I'm American also," I volunteered. I studied her face.

"Did you ever live in Maryland?" asked Elise.

"Never," I said. This was true.

"I used to travel a lot for my job. I worked as a student retention consultant."

It clicked. She *had* seen me. Elise had hosted a symposium at the university I had worked at. I remembered I'd left early—it was interesting stuff, but I wasn't really the right person from student services to be there, and I was burnt out. I'd sat by the door, thinking about how I didn't *have* to be there as we headed into the last session of the day.

When there was a slight pause, I had headed for the exit. Elise had said, "Ah, perhaps we need to work on retaining *meeting* participants as well."

I had said, "I'm sorry. I have to pick up my daughter."

She had smiled at me. "I'll have the administrative assistant put the packet in your box," she had said.

"Thank you," I had said. I didn't have to pick up my daughter, and I didn't have a box. Only teaching staff had a box.

Suddenly I was scared. America is a vast place, and the distance between there and where I sat at Yasemin's wooden table was far, but one thing I'd never thought about was the relative smallness of academia, the fascination of Western academics with the East, and the way these people were trained to remember faces and names and affiliations.

Could she have heard of what I'd done?

I stamped out my cigarette and quickly lit a fresh one.

"I always thought student retention was extremely important," I said. "I worked for a while in the admissions office at a school in Utah." This was also not true, but it was the first relatively close state I'd never been to that I could think of.

"Oh!" said Elise. "I probably recognize you from a conference! I've done some work in enrollment management as well."

"I bet that's it," I said.

I looked at my nails, which were ragged from kitchen and other work.

"Elise is always finding people she knows," said her husband.

The Austrians were absorbed completely in their own conversation. Yasemin was watching me. I saw that she had taken a cigarette from their pack and was puffing on it sternly.

"Where were you in Utah?" asked the wife of their friends.

"BYU at Provo," I said. It was the only school I immediately associated with Utah, and whether it was fair or not, I made a hasty guess that people in the even *smaller* world of religiously driven schools might not want to come to a Muslim country, so Elise might not have ever worked there.

"Oh," said the wife. "I have a friend at Weber State but I don't know anyone at BYU."

Thank Christ, I thought. Then, *Praise Allah*.

We finished the meal, Yasemin and I cleared, and our guests stumbled off.

"I don't think you ever worked in Utah," Yasemin said to me in the kitchen. She pronounced the state like *Oo-tah*. I was scrubbing a pan.

"Was it that bad?" I asked.

"*Hayır*," she said. "No. But I see you touch your finger when you lie. At the place where a woman could wear a ring." I could feel that she was looking at me, but I focused on the pan.

"I'm not wearing a ring," I said.

"I know," she said. "I can see."

"I'll finish the washing," I said.

"It is both of our work," Yasemin said. "Just know, I keep secrets. I won't tell your pink lies."

Pink lies. I smiled. "In English it is 'white' lie." I wasn't correcting her. I turned to face her. She was halfway in the pantry, organizing.

She shrugged. "Maybe these are different kinds of lies," she said.

Maybe.

•

In the morning, I overslept. When I finally woke, I saw that I had another text message from Paul.

ANKARA! ANKARA! ANKARA! read the screen.

I went to the kitchen, embarrassed by last night and by my bed head, and looked for tea.

"*Günaydın*," said Yasemin. She had the kettle on.

"Good morning," I said.

"Today is not a busy day or I would have knocked at your door," she said. "Today we are empty. So Elise is gone. That can be good news for you."

"Empty?"

"I have some reservations for tomorrow. Today, I think, we should forget this place and go to the *hamam*. We should celebrate your first—is it called a pay?"

I was startled. "You mean when a worker gets money? Payday."

"Payday. We celebrate your payday."

Yasemin handed me a well-used envelope and smiled.

"I want you to stay for a while, *canim*," she said.

I drank my tea, and a while later, Yasemin met me at the door to my room. We took the long way to the hammam wandering through the markets, and I walked past a heavy chain with many glass *nazar boncuğu*, a circle of deep blue with smaller circles and a black dot inside of it, clipped to it. It was meant to ward off the evil eye, to give protection, and to keep the wearer immune to gossip, spells, and general bad luck. It was a common symbol, and above the doorframes at her place, Yasemin had painted these everywhere. I liked the way my orange curtains flashed in the two small windows on either side of the door, with the *nazar* centered above it, like an anchor.

But when I walked past the vendor in the market, the chain crashed to the paving stones with a sound like a scream.

Yasemin tried to calm him in Turkish, but the seller only looked at me in disbelief, and as I bent to help him pick up the chips of cobalt glass, he shooed me off into the street, saying *dokunme, dokunme*, don't touch, don't touch.

When I'd made the call to my husband, I'd been prepared for anger or even indignation. What I knew was his sheer sadness, and my complete inability to help him understand why I hadn't come back, made me really sorry, maybe for the first time.

As I watched the chips of blue eye being swept into a bin, I thought I finally might understand what my absence must be like for him. It was not just that something was gone. It was also picking up the mess and piecing the larger fragments—like our daughter, our home—back together. I thought of how a bead of glue might fuse some of the hunks of glass, and how in the right light, it might be hardly noticeable. In the full sun, though, the seam would glow, and the first thing anyone would see would be the hasty patch job, the ragged mark of the scar.

Yasemin moved me along.

"Come," she said. "You must wash."

•

The first feeling was the feeling of heat.
The second, that of salt.

The Pull of It

Even before our clothes were off and we were in the full steam of the bathhouse, my sweat had begun to rise.

Yasemin disrobed in a second—for all their public modesty, in the cloister of the hamman, village women seem especially quick with getting their clothes off.

I took my time. She didn't seem to care. This was not a hurrying place.

My tattered American clothes, piled on the bench.

My light skin, beading with sweat.

The first room was crowded with lockers. There were several other women around, a few small girls with them. They did not look at me or at Yasemin, just towel-dried their hair and chatted.

"None of these women like me," she said.

I was surprised at her frankness.

"They don't speak English," she said. "Don't worry. I know them."

I followed her into the rooms of the hammam. I'd been in health club saunas before, and it wasn't that different, though the light was brighter and the steam hotter. The rooms were tiled in stone and all fanned out around the center, like the petals of a daisy. Water ran through channels cut in the stone, and there were some basins that collected water from open spigots before it ran onto the floor and back down the brass drains.

I wondered, in this arid place, where it all went and came from. River water diverted from irrigation ditches? And then back to the fields?

We sat near a basin. My hair was already soaked from humidity, and my lungs were beginning to feel suppler. At first I coughed from all the smoking I had been doing, but then deep breaths came easier and easier.

Still, sometimes I wondered how long I would stay. My ninety-day tourist visa would not last forever.

We sat. So much waiting.

"What do we do now?" I asked Yasemin.

"You should sit with your thoughts. Later we will wash. Traditionally people are coming to the *hamam* before they pray."

I liked this.

It was rare that I saw her without her scarf, and I was always surprised at how much hair she had. My own hair was thin, and if there was one American convenience that I really missed, it was ready access to a blow dryer. They were not hard to find, but the electricity went out so often, and the breakers were so ready to fail, that the vanity hardly seemed worth it.

As we sat longer, I could feel my skin softening under the teeth of the heat. I wondered how I looked. Other women filed in and they greeted each other, but no one said a word to Yasemin. She didn't seem to care, and she sat with her head tilted back against the stone with her eyes closed and her brown curls dripping over her shoulders and across her chest.

I wondered about her and her past life as a chemistry student and as the lover of other wive's men.

I wondered why she stayed in the village, when she said the village women did not like her. For the first time, I realized that the boardinghouse probably suffered too, because Yasemin did not tip the barkers at the bus stops who might then point tourists in her direction, and the restaurant proprietors likely did not recommend her either.

Yet she was calm.

Rooted. It was something deeper than having a community around, because she didn't. It was the place, I thought, that held her. Yasemin cradled in the valley, with the mountains rising toward the sky. The peaks punctured the sky and brought on violent weather, and Yasemin stayed still, her loop of chores and routines orbiting around her. I liked her gravity, and I liked how she refused to leave this small town where her parents were buried and where she'd been born.

Her hair pooled around her and steam rose from the crown of her head like an aura.

I wished I could read it.

•

The person I missed from home most was Anne, our daughter; leaving her made the least sense. Sometimes when I would hear about women giving up custody or sending their children to live with relatives, I would wonder what was wrong with them. I would think, *This child came from your body.* I would think, *It's like cutting off an arm.* It felt the same way now, and I wondered what was wrong with *me*, though at the same time I could also imagine scenarios where I might cut off my own arm—pinned beneath a boulder, trapped in a snarl of rope that was being tugged out to sea—and then the thought that while there would be some permanent loss, with enough nurture and rehabilitation, my shoulder would not hang empty forever.

My own parents were still together legally, but it would be a lie to say I felt the pull of the family. It had been so long since I had lived with them in my everyday life that each year ticking forward seemed to erase one off the back. I had thought when I had my own child that things would change—I was a little bit right. I understood my brothers better. They were younger than me but had both married early, and when Anne came I got, suddenly, why they'd dropped off.

I hadn't been that close with them anyway, and a little one takes so much time that the choice of what to do with any spare moment suddenly seems precious.

Even though he was the one that I called when I couldn't take my flight home, the last time I'd seen my brother Richard it hadn't gone that well.

Richard was the youngest, the last of our parents' three children, living in Bismarck. A buddy of his whom he'd played with in a fledgling band had moved there from Washington after high school because of some relatives and the promise of a job. He had always loved music and he followed his friend, packing his guitar into the back of a rotten Celica, and heading in the opposite direction as the pioneers. Not that their westward wagon tracks had ever done much for him.

They tried to perform for a while. When I spoke to him by phone, then, Richard was working as a dishwasher and drinking a lot, it sounded like. Once in a while he'd put down the phone and strum me something on his guitar, singing self-consciously in the kitchen of his studio apartment. I could never really hear him, but I'd close my eyes and listen hard for what I thought he might be trying to say.

It turned out that Bismarck was not the best place to launch from, and I don't think they were ever very good to begin with. A couple years later, he was working as a custodian at the state capital and engaged. I went to their small wedding in a city park, where we all toasted our beer cans to them.

Richard looked nice in a navy sport coat and khakis; his bride wore a simple summer dress. I had gone on a few dates with Julian by then, but I wasn't sure of where we were going.

That night, I had sex with my brother's best friend in the back of a pickup—it was thrilling and country and the flannel shirt he put under my head smelled like home.

Richard was very angry with me when he found out, and I wished I could tell him, my brother, that he actually had what I wanted. Surrounded by the golden grass of the plains and men with strong arms and ragged boots, his life seemed simple, like our childhood.

It seemed clean.

I thought it was what Daniel and I could have had, if we'd figured it out.

After Richard's first baby came, a few years later, he and his bride drove to eastern Washington to see our parents, and they did the extra miles across the state to see us in Seattle.

They'd been on the road with a four-month-old, and I wanted it to be nice for them; things had gotten serious with Julian by then, and we had married, but Anne had not yet arrived.

I made up the guest room, and I thought it looked very neat. I put the good guest sheets on the bed, yellow linen. Julian cooked dinner and Richard's wife insisted on doing the dishes. I tried to chat with my brother. He was tired from driving and visiting, but we made our way through several beers. The baby slept.

"How're Mom and Dad?" I asked him. It was summer and we were on the front porch, smoking. Sneaking cigarettes with him seemed like one of the only things we might still have in common.

"They seem old," he said.

The next day, we went out around Seattle—to the market and to Alki beach, and we picked our way along the waterfront. We had lunch at Julian's favorite restaurant and had espresso afterward.

Maybe I was smug.

Maybe I was so unhappy even then that I was pretending to my brother. I should have tried to talk more to his wife, Lisa. She might have been able to tell me something. She'd been working before, but now she stayed home with their boy. I thought the trip was a financial stretch for them, so Julian and I paid for everything.

I thought we'd all had a good time.

They spent one more night before packing up for their twenty-four hour drive back to Bismarck. Lisa was lying down and Richard was packing the car.

"It was good to see you," I told him. "I'm glad you came."

He looked like he was thinking.

"You know, Laura," he said, "you don't got it made. You're living out here with a fancy house and eat fancy food, and I don't see nothing here that seems like you."

His best man, all those years ago, had been gentle when he laid me out. His truck had a canopy on it, and he'd unrolled a sleeping bag for me and then crawled out to help me in. He had rough hands but he was tender with them.

"Okay," I said.

The best man had said something funny to me. He said, "Richard didn't think you would be here. He thought your other brother and your folks would come, but not you. Turned out to be the opposite."

"They don't like to travel. And it's summer, so they always worry about leaving the house because there might be fires."

"People are funny," he had said.

"I mean it," Richard was saying. "I think you turned out to be a liar."

"Richard," I told him, "I think I've always been a liar."

He thought about this. "Remember when Shelly Gerber's parents had that party, and she pushed me over the bank into the reservoir?"

"Yes," I said.

"You were the first person in the water after me. There were people all over the banks, but it was you who came in. You didn't even get your shoes off. I remember because your feet were wet the rest of the day."

"That was stupid of me," I said. "Shoes are hard to swim in."

"I would have died if you hadn't jumped after me."

"Someone else would have," I said. "You would have been okay."

"I don't know," he said.

In fact, that was the second time that Richard had almost drowned. He was a very good swimmer—we all were—but easily startled. The first time we'd been on a motorized boat and he'd leaned too far over the edge. When he hit the water, I screamed, and the driver, our uncle, turned around directly. Richard was wearing a life vest, but he'd landed face down. It was I who plucked him out, choking on pond water and fear.

I also didn't know if the second time it had to be me. I do remember hearing the *thunk* of a dead weight against liquid; I do remember looking to see who else had heard. The sun was already shining but it got brighter, so bright, like the contrast on a television screen turned so far up the faces are only a white blur. He was not thrashing, just slowly bobbing lower. I remember calling to him. I remember that he did not call back, and I dove.

"You didn't have to do nothing, Laura. No one else did nothing," he said.

There was commotion by the time we'd gotten back to the edge of the reservoir; the side he'd been pushed from was a blasted-out rock, and I'd had to drag him across the length of it where there was a low, grassy bank we could get out on. Our parents were there.

Shelly Gerber was there, looking sheepish. I wanted to punch her in the face, but I was too tired from swimming with one arm looped around Richard and from wearing my waterlogged shoes.

"I was scared too," I told him.

"No, you weren't," he said. "You were pissed."

"You're right," I said.

"I don't get why you aren't pissed now. Don't get me wrong; Julian is an okay dude, but if I'd thrown him off the docks yesterday you wouldn't have gone in."

"You wouldn't throw him off the docks," I said. I tried to imagine the two wrestling on the pier.

"I might've. I didn't think you'd be the kind of woman who stays with some guy because he has a little money or a few nice things. My sister hated people like that," he said.

So much, so direct. It wasn't like Richard. I wondered what he'd seen in me.

When we were children, we had clung to one another and our brother. We made a wall of dirty faces and tiny limbs against the gray world of adults.

When I was underwater, air meant nothing to me, only Richard, and I swam hard toward him, surfacing at his back and then lacing my arm around him.

When he took off his shirt, the best man looked fragile. I opened to him.

Lisa was at the car now, and I hugged her awkwardly, trying not to bump the car seat. Julian waved from the porch.

If I reached now, who would reach back?

•

Yasemin had brought soap and rags to perform *kese*, a special kind of washing where the cloth is coarse and the rubbing is hard enough to actually slough off the first dead layer of skin. She showed me how to do it, and then she did my back and the other places I couldn't reach.

Soaking in the wet air of the *hamam*, the skin softens and peels away easily in little white rolls. *Kese* looks a little gruesome but it doesn't hurt while it's happening.

What hurts is after, when the new pink skin is exposed. When Yasemin tossed a dipper of hot water on me to rinse, there was a sting like deep sunburn.

I tried not to let Yasemin see me wince, but my whole body flinched.

"Now me," she said and turned her back toward me.

I took the cloth and scrubbed her with pressure, like she had told me.

I rinsed her and then we washed again, this time with gentle, foaming soap.

We sat for a while longer and then headed back to the lockers. The other women still avoided Yasemin's eyes and they avoided mine. We dried and changed into fresh clothes.

I covered my wet hair, and we stepped into the brisk air.

I felt glad for this new, clean skin, and on the short walk back to Bahçe Evi, I thought of Richard and everything swirled.

In the night, I had what felt like a Daniel dream, but it was only me and Anne. We had to make it to the caves, but I didn't know the way. The beasts and the fowl watched for someone to lead, as they stamped their hooves and exhaled great puffs of steamy breath, but they weren't looking to me. My daughter would take us.

•

It wasn't the first time.

Anne was three, and I told Julian I was leaving.

"Why?" he asked. "I didn't see this."

It was harder to explain than I expected. The ideas were there, but I had a hard time getting the words out of my mouth. I had wondered if he had thought of the first time, when I'd gone before, when he drove me to the airport and my plane zipped across the Atlantic.

Four years would have passed. Enough to get over the immediacy of something, but not so long that it would be forgotten.

"I need to make a change," I had said then, frustrated at how this sounded, like the sound of a spoon against a pan, hollow, metallic.

"Could we try counseling?" he asked. I knew Julian liked solutions.

"We could," I said. "But not now." I also liked solutions, but solutions are like cheese—it takes time for the wetness to press out; it takes time for it all to cure.

We were naked, just getting out of bed. In fact, this nakedness was part of a problem—we were so casual about it all the time that I'd look at household things, like a jumble of boxes in the garage that never made it to the Goodwill, and I'd look at my husband's sex, and each seemed equally as ordinary and unimportant.

"I'm not asking for a divorce," I told him. "I just need some time."

Thunk.

Pull.

"You plan to come back," he said. It was helpful for me to hear Julian talk in this way, in statements; he spoke often to confirm or disconfirm. He had swung his legs over the side of the mattress and pulled his robe from the row of hooks above his nightstand.

I hesitated. "I think so. Yes."

I knew that my husband could stay very calm in crises. For example, in an earthquake, he would be the one who would know which doorways were load bearing, and therefore the best to take shelter under. If trapped in debris, he would actually have a whistle with which to alert rescuers. He would produce this from his pocket, along with water purification tablets, flares, high-protein snacks, and compress bandages. He would also, despite perhaps being pinned to wreckage, be able to reach his pocket to retrieve these items, and he would know not to actually light the flares, lest the spark of a match ignite the combustibles from ruptured gas lines.

"What about Anne?" he asked.

When we had decided on the name Anastasia, we had followed the trend of giving girls old-fashioned names and then making the names cute, like Ellie for Eleanor, Abby for Abigail, and so on. He had not liked my idea that we could go with Dorky for Dorcas, even though I had a great aunt Dorcas. I was only partly joking. I thought it might make her tough.

"Dorcas means *gazelle*," I had told him.

"I like Gazelle better," he had said.

I put on a shirt and a pair of athletic pants. "I can't take her," I said. "I think she will be okay with just you for a while. She likes you."

"Of course she likes me," Julian said.

"Not all kids like their parents," I said. "But she likes you. You are lucky with that."

"She's only three. She doesn't know not to like me," he said.

"I doubt it," I said.

"This is strange, Laura," he said. "I feel like this is the first I've heard of it. I feel like this is sudden." He cinched his robe. It was plaid.

I wanted to say, *I have tried to speak to you and you have elected not to listen.*

I wanted to say, *By the time you get home in the evening, I have had so much vodka that I don't care.*

I wanted to say, *Enjoy the second shift!*

I would have meant any of these things, but in truth, Julian was kind to me and to Anne, in an old-fashioned way—he came home late and often excused himself to our shared office to work some more, but I believed more that he had poor time management skills and a traditional man's allegiance to work than that he was actually avoiding us. And, I also wasn't sure how much any kind of explanation would be helpful. What could I say, really, to help explain why I did not want to wake up next to him for a while?

"Do you want some coffee?" he asked, always civil.

I nodded.

Julian tightened his robe again as he passed me, heading for the kitchen. I had given him the robe when we were new. In fact, I had stolen it from someone who I'd thought of as my last hurrah before settling into a serious life. I'd let the guy pick me up at a bar; he was dressed nicely with a pretty smear of gray around his temples. I still liked that look—someone who is just on the cusp of getting older. There is something about the turn away from youth that brings out our sex.

As Julian rummaged around in the kitchen—grinding the beans, measuring water—I remembered how I'd casually lifted the Nordstrom bag that held what was now my husband's robe on my way out of that stranger's house. There had been a gift receipt inside, and Julian had been ultimately too polite to exchange it even though the color was not exactly right for him.

After we had our coffee, awkwardly, and Julian went to work, I did leave. It was only for a week and a half, not enough to really amount to much. I went to Washington's Olympic Peninsula—the arm of the state that sticks out into the Pacific. On a map it looks like the edge of paper, torn with a bead of saliva down the crease instead of cut with scissors, ragged and wet. Also, it was October, so the water and the sand and the sky were all very gray.

I didn't do much but drink wine on the porch of a dumpy condo. I watched the blur of the surf into the coastline and clouds, and I considered how maybe same-ness did not have to mean stasis.

Then I went home, and when I unpacked my bag, I put it back in the closet in the same place, and I hung all of my clothes on the exact same hangers I had taken them from.

•

I refused to believe it was something about marriage. It was something about us and the everyday: the longer Julian and I were coupled, the more I developed an indifference to the body. We'd been passionate once, but increasingly, I thought of intimacy like the messes that were accumulating in more and more corners of our house. When we had first moved in, the immediacy of any kind of clutter was unbearable to me; later, it became inconvenient; finally, there was a settling.

We became like any other piece of household effluvia.

Here is the stove.

Here is the laundry.

Here is my breast.

It was almost like a miracle that we'd conceived Anne, not a sacred one, but one of statistics. I felt a kind of guilt about it, with so many people who struggled, who timed their copulations around ovulation, and injected themselves with the urine of a woman already with child.

Early in the pregnancy, I took down a framed painting from one wall in our office and leaned it

against the opposite wall. I was only going to move it—
it was too heavy in the original space and made the
room feel like it was tilting. When Julian asked me what
I was doing, he said that it was just me, that the room
was certainly not tilting.

"I said it *feels* like it is tilting," I told him, "not
that it is *actually* tilting."

"I don't see it," he said. "But I don't care if it
gets moved."

"Maybe you're used to it," I said. "Like people
who have one leg longer than the other and they never
really know until they go to a chiropractor because their
back hurts."

Julian gave me a blank look.

"They think it's their back because they're used
to the leg," I said, trying to explain.

"If one of my legs were longer than the other, I
would know," Julian said.

I gave him this. He was scientific like that; he
might have been right. He might have already measured.

"I'll let it sit for a few days," I said. "We can see
how it *feels*."

Years later, though, the painting remained un-
hung. His mother had given it to us; it had been in her
house for many years and had been bequeathed to us
with much ceremony. A landscape in a gold laminate
frame, it was the kind of thing that gets thrown out
when people pass, but for now it was with us.

Occasionally I would vacuum underneath and
behind it, where it was making an ever-deeper groove
against the plush. Sometimes I would even clean the

glass, but I got used to the way it looked in the office, and finally, Julian stacked a box of files in front of it.

Our collections, our dust in the atria.

Even after Julian's mother died we did not throw it out, as by then it had become another layer in our unsteady foundation, a sediment of glass and old shoes and dirty sheets, held together by nothing but static.

There were times that I thought having more regular sex with Julian would be like exercise or healthy eating or reading the classics or driving a stick-shift—things that can be hard to get started on but become easier with practice, stimulating even. Or like growing a vegetable patch; once the long wait for spring is over and the seeds have been started, the transplanting complete, the frequency of watering gauged, the garden is sustaining. The memory of crisp lettuce propels a whole host of other activities, like changing the design of the plot or contemplating the reproductive life of aphids.

Before I met him, I'd spent a year feeling either despondent or predatory. It was taking a lot of time to process Daniel, but then towards the end of it, a few months after I'd met Julian, miraculously I'd gotten the job in the Registrar's Office. All the smart people then were looking for jobs in tech, but I liked what I thought was the safety of an academic setting. It wasn't that I pursued anyone relentlessly or illegally or was especially horrible toward men, but I would meet them and I would sleep with them. I had so much energy for this and no energy for anything beyond it. Beyond the excitement of the casual, it was also the pitch of it: one clear note that did not sustain.

Once, when Julian and I were new, I bumped into him in line at a coffee shop. I had already been over to his apartment a few times by then. We hung out in the coffee shop for a while, and then because the day was so pretty we thought it might be worth it to go to the beach. My car, a hatchback with the rear seats perpetually down, was parked nearby, and after we'd had enough of walking through the cold sand, and after we'd stopped into a local place for a few cocktails, we ended up fucking in the back of my car.

"I didn't really mean to go that far," Julian said to me when we were done.

"Me neither," I said, but I had. I was young then, but I wasn't an idiot—I'd grown up on a farm, so I didn't believe these things just happened. I mean that I knew the pure pull of biology, because that even an old milk cow will dance around a little for the aging bulls if she is open, whether she can really carry a calf or not.

"Hey," I said. "It's not like it was my first time." I smiled.

By then I'd already had many of these kinds of lovers—these easy, couple-of-dates men. They were not difficult to find, especially because I was like them. Julian was different. He wasn't looking for just a screw.

As I saw more and more of him, he calmed me.

He was level.

Indeed, his legs were perfectly plumb.

Even though there was passion early on, our
courtship still felt habitual before habit even had time to
form.

When we said our vows quietly, at the courthouse, with no one but the state-appointed witnesses in
attendance, I took it all to be a sign of love—the inward
turn, the lack of declaration in the smell of the clerk's
triplicate papers, the understated legality. I thought this
was the other side of all those uncomplicated fucks—an
uncomplicated husband made with a simple signature.

I held Julian's hand on our way to a late lunch.
The April was misty.

I was a damp bride in bad shoes. The dim light
of the afternoon fell onto Julian from the side, and the
light off him was just as dim, like a prism without
enough angles to refract.

•

Later, I was pregnant with Anne, and when she
had grown enough for her features to come through
clear on a sonogram, I'd wondered if my husband was
really her father. By then, he was working as a policy
staffer at a big environmental organization. I hadn't
been unfaithful to him, but I did have trouble accepting
that this man of precision and exacting recycling
standards was really capable of fathering a girl with such
a fine, watery face.

It wasn't until the contractions came on
strong—after Julian's workday but before he had
changed out of his suit—that I was sure she was half his.
She was already a girl made of accidental impeccable

timing, a trait she would have gotten from him, so it seemed appropriate that she would come without inconvenience.

She arrived early in the morning, just as the spring sky was lighting up. I was surprised at how quickly they took her from me. There had been part of me that had wanted to have her at home, away from the chill of a hospital and aggressive scalpeling, but I had also, growing up, seen many births—mostly of cattle and swine—and more than making me comfortable with the idea, I was terrified. Though it usually doesn't, much can go wrong. There can be a great deal of screaming. There can be blood. I felt close to the idea that birth is a place where two worlds are opened at the same time. I was happy that Anne had come to us in the morning rather than in the twilight.

Julian decided that he would go to work directly, unshaven, and in the same clothes as the day before.

"You could stay here," I said to him. "Or you can go home."

"You should rest," he said. "And your mother will be here before too long." My mother had been driving through the night to meet her new grand-daughter.

"But they'll understand, Jules, if you take a day off," I said.

"I'm fine," he said. "I can get through my day."

It would only be fair to say that the kiss he planted on my forehead was sweet, that he closed the door gently on his way out. Julian was kind, and Julian was smart, but there were certain things he could not see.

I didn't want to sleep either, for the first time in too long. I wanted to be awake with him, with our new girl.

I understood that he needed the normalcy of his office, but I didn't like it.

As days went on, normalcy helped him take to parenting. We were assured sleepless nights were normal, and I breastfed normally: for a year, somewhere between the minimum requirements and the cutoff of getting too old for it in public. I took my maternity leave and then I went back and had the advantage of flex-time that places like universities offer, and I was appropriately grateful for the school's reasonable expectations of a mother employed outside the home.

Anne hit her developmental marks.

Julian started a consulting firm with a friend.

By the time we celebrated her second birthday, I had completely lost any ability I had left to get angry, about anything. Where I used to flare, I shrugged.

My brother Richard had seen it, those years ago when he had said the sister he remembered was a *pissed* sister.

So when I left Julian the first time, even for such a short duration, it wasn't out of rage. I hadn't been able to get mad at the way being a mother had changed my emotional life, and I hadn't had a chance to rail against the inequalities of female versus male parentage—really, I had it pretty easy. Really, there wasn't much for me to go on a tear about. But if there was, I couldn't feel it.

Mostly, it was hard for me to engage.

The household and my life with Julian had gone infestive, like zebra mussels or mint.

Grime in the ventricles, earth in the aorta.

I still had some friends, and I was deeply envious of most of them. I saw how instead of sinking into the dust bunnies of their more adult life, they'd warmed to it and kept the corners swept clear.

No beggar's velvet, no slut's wool.

Mostly, when I was gone from my husband and daughter, I missed my daughter. And from my perch on the condo porch at the seaside, I hoped that he would find her difficult.

I knew she would spend most of the time at daycare, which she liked. I knew that Julian would spend most of his time at his office, which he liked.

My first absence was also about him being more present with her, because he would have to. I wanted this both because I thought Anne deserved a present father, and because I didn't want Julian to think he could be spared the emotional life of girls. He didn't get to just disappear into his work. She was not a demanding child, but she was still a child, and there were things that needed to be done, like picking her up on time, and carefully combing her hair, and shielding her from the boring ugliness of adults.

When I came back, there was also the feeling that nothing had changed. I shouldn't say I came back. I should say I returned, this time with even less than what I'd left with. In the evenings, we still sat silently across from each other at the table, and we listened to our daughter chirp away about her day in the toddler language that only we three shared.

I had learned that I'd been wrong about my reasons for staying married to Julian. So far, I didn't know how to do anything about it. For years I had thought that his patience and his composure had been good for me. He had tamed me, and I thought this was trust.

Now I felt deeply dishonest.

I also thought I probably still knew the difference between the flash of heat that comes with infatuation and the enduring kind of devotion that can keep two lives together.

And Julian was very devoted. He could have easily filed papers at any time. He knew the kinds of people who were good at these things. I knew the kinds of people who drank too much in an attempt to self-medicate their ennui, and who called it such. Julian's friends had walls of dry cleaning protecting them against all the things that might really be going on; mine had their jobs with students in the sheltered world of nonprofits.

I wasn't entirely sure that having Anastasia had made me a better person. It had made me a different person. Without her, I might have been able to leave Julian for longer. Without her, I might also not have noticed how slow and predictable our patterns had become, how our blood had turned to dirt. Besides the dreams about Daniel, I didn't have a longing for my old life, but rather a deep reservation about where we were going.

I thought maybe I could finally put the picture back up or do some intense organizing—change the weight of the house, the slope of it.

Once, when I'd gotten new tires on my car, I'd seen the technician wedge little lead weights between the rim and the rubber. Julian described to me the difference between static and dynamic balance and that most shops were converting to zinc instead of lead because of the environmental impact.

Very simple and clever; I needed some of these.

Scraps of something hard to lace into the wobbly bits to smooth me if there ever came a time of increasing speed.

CHAPTER FOUR

It wasn't until spring was past new and the violent green of the new shoots had started to turn to the harder leaves that would survive through summer that the host of insects appeared, many of which I was sure I hadn't seen before. The climate in central Turkey was not so different than what I'd grown up with, but the bugs were, or seemed to be, so all week long I'd been taking pictures of the hatchlings on the front steps to the room of the boardinghouse where I lived and worked. Paul had come by, briefly, one day, and left me a camera with a manual wind, and I liked the action of it. I imagined the *snap* of the shutter having the same force as a mandible, and I clicked through the series of insects like the cracking of a jaw.

But when I took my film to a lab, most of the prints came back purely black with the developer's white border. By the time I flipped through the last of the photos, I had decided that I would accept the invitation Paul had extended to go with him to Ankara. It was strange to me that in the entire country I didn't know anyone beyond him and Yasemin.

Clearly, I thought, *the entomological life is not working for you.* Nor was the isolation: it was all reflected back to me in black. I put the failed pictures with the others and arranged the time off.

When I was an early teenager, I had decided, over an ambitious summer, that I would memorize the capitals of countries worldwide. States were accounted for, in school. The Canadian provinces checked off, due to the fact that my family lived closer to Canada than what we called the *other* Washington, Washington D.C. I don't think I realized then the *estados* of Mexico and contented myself with being able to name Mexico City (how easy, like Oklahoma City!) before moving on to South America, and then farther east. I grew up in a small town, and I believed that college was my ticket out; I was right about this, even though I learned later I was extremely wrong about what admissions committees might care about, and after I had worked in one, I regretted no one had told me there was no reason not to apply to brand-name private schools.

My parents had two sets of encyclopedias, an authoritative set of *The Encyclopædia Britannica* and the friendlier, better-illustrated *World Book*. I had these outdated volumes spread around me as I made my way around the Mediterranean, and when I got to Turkey, I recited *On-CAR-a, On-CAR-a*. How different it sounded in the mouth of Turks, with the emphasis on the first syllable. At busy bus stations, the attendants called it out like Paul's text message, the first I had ever received: *AN-kara, AN-kara, AN-kara!*, like a chant or a mantra, not a simple destination on the inter-city lines.

Paul was working on a new installation project, so he had been passing through more often, collecting rocks and bags of red dirt. The last time I had seen him, he'd asked Yasemin if he could look through the old tool shed on her property, and when he emerged triumphantly with a rusted scythe he offered to pay her for it, and she laughed.

"Only the American wants to buy garbage," she said. "Take it."

She helped him wrap it in some old flour sacks and cardboard so that he would not be denied entry onto the bus, a *yabancı* with a blade.

"Actually the villagers will know this is not a weapon," she said to him as she tied twine around the bulky package.

"Even in Kayseri I think they would know," said Paul. "Even I know."

"*Evet*," she said. "But it doesn't look good, and you know, sometimes you are doing things that are strange. People see."

"Like what?" Paul asked.

"Like you get on the minibus with this *tırpan* and your stones."

"I think she's right," I said to Paul. "It doesn't look good."

That last time he was at the boardinghouse, he had stashed the scythe for a while and we went to my porch to drink some wine. We had killed more than a few bottles on the steps, under the glow of the orange curtains and the protection of the *nazar*, but Paul had never crossed the threshold into my room.

"It's beautiful here," he said, "but it's good to get out."

I wasn't sure how I would feel about him if I had met him in America. The United States always seemed so vast and sprawling while I was there (how could Honolulu and Helena be in the same country?), but away from the place, I was suddenly moved by nationalism. It wasn't that I felt patriotic, but I considered the commonalities in a way I hadn't before.

Given her expanse, in fact, there's often little else Americans have in common besides being American. And there is an understanding, too, which many people who are living away from their country share—they have the secrets of why they've left and what they've left behind, and their footing is not always sure, navigating without a strong grasp of language or customs or home.

"I'll go," I told him. "I haven't seen Ankara. I got the time off from Yasemin."

"So I'll see you again in a few days," he said.

Was this what I had left my husband and my daughter for? To wait with a man who was not my husband to catch the early bus, where we would sit, legs touching, for five hours? After America, it was strange to know so many people who did not have cars. It was strange not to have one.

Paul had taken a connection so that he could meet me at the bus station, and he was there when I showed up with unwashed hair and my daypack, the only bag I owned. I liked the way the morning time was moving slowly. We smoked while we waited, and when we lit cigarettes, the flame from the match came up in gradual ignition, the smoke curled, our exhaled breath pooled like fog around us.

I thought, *I am going to Ankara only to talk to the consulate and get my visa renewed.*

It was true the visa was something I needed to address. It was expired. I had the credit card.

I wore the set of silver spiral earrings that had been getting dusty on the narrow ledge above my sink.

We milled around, ashed our cigarettes, and toed at the dirt. Even though a lot of vehicles came through to drop off travelers, the town did not have a proper structure. We stood among the attendants wrangling passengers onto the correct coaches, seats emptying and filling again.

"I wish I had some coffee," Paul said.

"Me too," I said.

I wondered at the vows I had taken.

In sickness, in health.

Was not knowing how to return a sickness? Sometimes I thought, *Yes*, and sometimes I thought, *Don't patronize me*, and sometimes I thought, *I'm on my way to the cure!*

And besides the Americanism, somewhere between making the decision not to get my flight back—and then, doing my best to disappear into the interior of a country that was not my own—and meeting Paul, I had become compressed.

He had a spouse too, logging long hours like Julian did.

When the bus came, we boarded in a pair.

I took the morning as a gift.

•

The buses were as civilized as I remembered. We were fed tea and small cookies and offered cologne scented with lemon to keep our hands fresh. On the way to Ankara, it seemed like even the inevitable piles of crumbled plaster and shattered pottery, the heaps of plastic and rusted olive oil tins, were glittering.

This is what travel does.

This is in part what had turned me against returning as scheduled. Maybe I had an overdeveloped sentimentality toward garbage too, but it is also true that sometimes the light falling from a different part of the sky is truly illuminating.

Even the ants mining at a dried-up orange peel seemed large and busy. They appeared to be doing something important. It therefore becomes extremely curious as to why a person, with so many more cells and sophisticated tools, should be living a life that is such a colossal bore.

In any city there will be trash, but to me Ankara was already more like the spark of sun against smashed glass and less simple urban debris.

I thought back to my capitals.

For better or for worse.

I would have said I was sorry, if anyone had asked me, to leave my daughter behind, but I also would have said that I hoped by the time she was my age that she would never have to understand what compels a person to do so.

For part of the way, I slept. The seats were comfortable, his body close. When Paul and I got off of the bus at the large terminal, he led me through the maze of vendors selling snacks and souvenirs to the local metro.

"Green line," he said, referring to the two train routes that intersected at some points, including the major bus stations, "always take the green line. Don't ever get on the red. It doesn't go anywhere."

In fact, even I knew the English translation for the word labeling the red line: *havalimanı*. The red line ended at the airport.

And then it was all at once, in a flash: the crush of bodies on the train, the cars clacking and speeding into the city. It was May by now, and it had just been announced that the current parliament would be dissolved and a new one put into office in November. There were riot police out the window, because this news had charged the upcoming local elections; they lined up with their awkward Plexiglas shields. I was used to seeing groups of youths—and both the demonstrators and the black-clad police were young—from working on campus, but I was not used to the flak-jackets and the signs in looping Arabic script held by the Islamists against the signs with Marxist slogans written in English, German, French, and Turkish.

Yet, the police looked calm. The demonstrators animated but contained. Paul was crammed into the seat next to me, our packs on our laps. I felt the warmth of his leg next to mine, I smelled the thick of tobacco on my hair, my jacket, my skin, and I almost went for his hand. Almost.

The day was bright. The train rode smoothly and was just crowded enough that it made me aware of the people around me. The light was flattering— everyone looked like they had life still in them, not like they'd just come hardscrabble out of the villages or from pockets of the inner neighborhoods. Even the communists and the covered women, outside, rallying with the other parties, looked gorgeous, lit by the mid-spring sun and idealism.

"I don't think I've ever seen a real, card-carrying Party member," I said to Paul.

"Trotsky lived in Istanbul for a while," he said.

"In exile," I said. I remembered this from somewhere, and I was pleased with myself.

"In Büyükada," he said. "It's an island. We could go there. There are no cars allowed, only bikes and horses."

"I'm allergic to horses," I said. This was true.

"Bikes too?" he asked.

"Certainly not," I said and adjusted on the plastic seat, inching perhaps a centimeter closer to him.

"Then we could go," he said.

Our stop was not far. I followed him through the downtown district, Kızılay, and waited while he bought us both another bus fare.

I loved the back of Paul's blond head. And I loved that he seemed to be forever getting a ticket of some kind.

We took another short ride and got off at the top of a hill, walked for a few blocks, and went into the lobby of an apartment building. When Paul's friend Mehmet let us in, his flat was so warm I turned almost immediately to mush—it was not a cool enough day to really need heat, even if Turks are perpetually cold and believe the cold brings all kinds of illnesses, from simple flu to heart disease. *He must be rich*, I thought, because heat was expensive and generally sporadic. I would learn later that Mehmet was not rich. He worked at the

Ministry of Culture. It was only Ankara, land of concrete and central heating. Yasemin was right: it gleamed.

This was another different world.

For one, there was less religion and more beer.

It was Friday, the Muslim holy day, and in Göreme, most things would be closed, at least for noon prayers. My day off. It was an important stop on the tour maps because of the interesting geology and pastoral farmlands, but there weren't a lot of places to get a drink, especially if the all-tourists-all-the-time discos didn't sound appealing. The state-run liquor store stayed open, which I knew from finishing quite a few bottles of local wine on my steps, alone, just like in America.

It had been a long time since I'd been to a nightclub. I was over thirty, married, and had a young child.

I was shocked when Paul suggested it.

"I don't think I have the right clothes," I said.

"You're dressed fine," said Paul. "It's mostly bands playing cover music."

"Cover bands," I said.

"Yes. You know, bands that play the music from other bands," said Mehmet.

"I understand 'cover bands,'" I said.

Okay, I thought. Cover bands. *This is something people do. I can do this.* I thought of Yasemin as a girl in Ankara, this new world.

Platinum, silver, tungsten.

"Laura," Paul said, "mostly people here just dance. It's not clubbing to be seen."

"I'm in my village jeans," I said. *Mom jeans,* I thought. *Closer-to-forty-than-I-want-to-admit jeans.* I was glad I at least had on a necklace, and that my glasses sort of hid that there was no makeup around my eyes.

"A true village women doesn't wear jeans," Mehmet said. "You're fine."

We took a taxi, and it was such an urban pleasure, piled between two men, swerving through the crowded streets that flanked the high-rises.

It was a short trip, dodging through the busy sidewalks, and then up a flight of stairs. One step into the bar and the music was like diving into cold water—a chilly shimmer, a caught breath—and then coming up for air. Paul came back and put a clammy beer in my hand; Mehmet took my other hand and twirled me across the sticky floor, alcohol sloshing and guitar pounding.

A country of dance fanatics, both drunken and holy.

I forgot all about being shy about my pants, and I closed my eyes so I could better feel the bass line. The band was very bad, but I knew the songs, and after a few more drinks I was pushed close to the stage and hollering the choruses, just like I used to.

Will you honor and keep him?

I would dance by myself until Paul or Mehmet spun me, and I swirled with them, boozy and happy.

Later in the night, Paul went off. He had had too much to drink, as had I. I think that I probably already knew, at least in part, what his trips to Ankara were about, but it wasn't until I saw him dancing with a pretty Turk (she was even cuter than the collective whole of the communists) that it was confirmed.

I was reasonably alert, not sober, but sober enough to know what I was up to, when I leaned into Mehmet, who looked familiar but who was still a stranger.

Like the men from so long ago.

Maybe this is why I stayed out of the bars.

It's been so nice to meet you, I said, putting my lips on his cheek as I came away from his ear. You too, he said, and he kissed me lightly back.

I took a break for the restroom and to get some more beer, and in the moments when I was hovering over the pissy squat toilet before I returned to Mehmet, I tried to parse why I was so angry at Paul, and all I could come up with was that I wasn't upset that he took weekend trips to dance with younger women, I was upset that he had been picking them over me, even though I was not available to be chosen.

He is not your husband, I reminded myself. *You are his guest and we are friends and that is all.*

I lingered at the bar on the way back, and when I could not stop seeing Paul's head bob above the crowd, I watched out the window, where four stray dogs were attacking an alley cat. They grabbed it in their mouths, one paw for each, and they pulled until the cat ceased to struggle, until one leg came neatly off and fur was tufted on the dirty pavement, and then they left the body without a taste of the blood. The dogs did not go off in a pack, just licked themselves and scooted down different alleys.

Forsaking all others.

And that is how I found myself waking up Saturday morning wrapped in Mehmet's long legs.

When I pulled myself out of his bed, I wished for the camera. I wished for my private porch-life and a katydid. I imagined a shot of Mehmet, his thinning black hair like the back of a beetle.

I went to look for Paul, who was smoking in the living room. "Did you sleep?" he asked.

"Sort of," I said. "I'm a little hung over."

"Me too," he said. "Come with me to the kitchen. I'll make you a Nescafé."

He got up from the couch and with one hand held his cigarette, while the other very lightly touched my waist.

"I heard you come back in early this morning," I said.

He nodded and moved his hand.

Paul heated water in the kettle, and we stood drinking our instant coffees in the kitchen. Mehmet roused. We listened to him shower and we smoked. Paul heated more water.

"I can make some breakfast," I said.

"It's okay," Paul said. "We can go out. You cook enough in that place you work."

"I like the place where I work," I said.

"Good," Paul said.

Mehmet's steps were on the floor and then he poked his head into the kitchen.

"I've got to go vote," he said.

"Who is your party?" Paul asked.

"I'm planning on voting for DEHAP, the Kurdish party," he said.

"Oh, okay," I said. This was what I said when I knew nothing about a topic.

Mehmet left, and Paul opened the refrigerator. He was not wearing a shirt and all down his back were scars—once he had mentioned having to have moles removed—and I thought of the decency of it, to wear his wounds on the outside. I wanted to touch each one, but decided it was like pointing out a hole in somebody's clothes, only worse.

Like *The Film*, I thought, the credits to Paul's life would be superimposed on a hanging side of beef. Alongside, I was firecrackers in the fog and the hope they were not gunshots.

•

DEHAP and the Kurds did not win the Ankara elections. This much was clear even before the polls had closed. They earned a few seats, but nothing that resembled a majority. I didn't follow Turkish politics, so I wasn't sure if this was important or not. Mehmet came back to the apartment with a thick smear of black on his thumb from the voting booth.

"We use a fingerprint because even in Ankara there are some people who can't write," he told me.

I was amazed, and later, after Paul went out on some undescribed errand, I let Mehmet fuck me again. I found a smear of ink across my hip.

•

The ride back was slow. I hadn't made it to the consulate to check on my visa. I insisted that I was fine, but even though Paul could have gotten on a direct bus to Kayseri, he took the connection again so that I would not be by myself.

"It's five hours," he said. "It gets boring."

We'd done a lot of walking around town and I was tired. I thought to myself the slogan I had seen—in English! I was excited!—on the back of a Fiat angle-parked on one of the streets we'd walked through: *Go Slime a Salmon, Visit Alaska,* and I remembered the quick rip of gutting a fish: slice the belly and in one swipe tear out the innards, leave the meat. I couldn't remember in what order the head was supposed to come off or if, maybe, it didn't until later.

Either way my thoughts wouldn't clear.

In joy as well as sorrow.

There were still updates coming in from the elections. I could hear the bursts of voices and static from the radio at the front of the bus, and occasionally the riders in the forward seats would clap or groan and then the porter would make an announcement over the public address speakers.

"How did the communist party do?" I asked Paul. His Turkish was very good.

"There's nothing about them," he said. "They are not popular."

"You know, I was very upset with you," I said to him. "But I'm not now."

"I know," he said.

155

I thought of when I had been riding the Ankara metro with Paul, and how he had said that we were like sperm headed toward the egg, no choice in destination. And upon departure, that morning, that the tunnel was a birth canal, and there we were just waiting to be puked into the open air. He was contradictory on this point: whether we were headed in or out.

Maybe the direction wasn't the point.

Keep yourself unto him.

Maybe the important point was the zoom, the steady motion of wheels, and being carried on something we could not steer ourselves.

We were quiet for the remainder of the ride, and when the bus arrived at my town, Paul got off to make his transfer. I remembered how back in Ankara we had been walking around, and while crossing the street I had nearly stepped in front of a *dolmuş*. Paul and Mehmet were already through the intersection, and I was choking on the diesel fumes and starting to understand how I had to be in this country, where there was no one to pull me back from the crowded streets full of fatalistic drivers or a high, open window.

Back at the boardinghouse, there was a moth couple communing by the door casement. I had a fresh roll of film, so I went directly to load the camera to try and capture them in the last of the dying light.

By the time I got back outside, one was trapped in a spider's web.

The other's fate, it seemed, was unclear.

•

I wanted to talk to my daughter, so I walked to the phone booth to call her at my parents' house, being careful of the time. It was late for me, but they would be just getting ready for school, if I had counted correctly, if she were still there and not back with Julian. I hated thinking of her going to the same, small-town school I'd attended, but I took deep breaths. She was smarter than me, more social in some ways, more inward in others. Better. She would be okay.

The rings were slow and long, but no one answered. Then, I dialed Julian, and nothing. I didn't leave a message. I thought of trying Daniel, my lover from so long ago, my childhood friend. The digits to his parents were at the tip of my fingers, a number I could not forget if I tried.

I was reaching, for anyone, but I stopped.

There were too many already—Daniel, Julian, Paul, now Mehmet—when I really wanted Anastasia and my mother. I wanted to go back to the boarding-house and rouse Yasemin and stay up even later, talking with her in the quiet.

Out of the phone booth, my feet were heavy in the Anatolian dust.

For the first time, I felt the deep place Daniel had been rooted in start to move, slipping, giving me a little more room.

Once in an in-between place, when Julian and I had been dating, but also fighting—just disagreements and picking, I think we'd been spending too much time together—I was walking with Julian and was sure I saw Daniel. Still, I think it was him. Julian and I were doing something ordinary, paying for parking, and then there was this reminder, a body, a person, sloping along the sidewalk and pretending not to notice.

Or maybe he really didn't see us.

I wasn't sure which was worse.

When I looked back, there were the early years with Julian, when I'd wake from a deep sleep and swear I smelled combustion ready to happen, like coal in a horn or propane blowing but not yet lit, and be almost surprised that it wasn't Daniel there with me.

One Halloween, Julian and I had thrown a party in one of our old apartments, and I woke to a scene of shredded balloons and feathers, soft carpet on my toes, pinched from wearing heels all night, and a man, passed out in the center of it, party debris like a halo all around him, and for a second, again I was sure it was Daniel, come to reclaim me, and I couldn't understand how I had missed him all night. Then I looked closer, and the features were wrong.

He was a boy, younger than my childhood friend and long ago lover would have been, and his skin a shade paler, but he was peaceful, sleeping there on our floor; he was someone who I wanted to curl up next to and fold against his chest.

I might have been thinking of doing this when Julian stumbled in and said, "Who's that?"

"I don't know," I said, admitting it. "Should we wake him?"

"I'll make coffee," Julian said. "Wait until then."

I remembered this, so polite, even to a stranger.

Some things were clear, but it was long enough ago that I did struggle to remember certain details. A decade. What had happened after Julian had got the coffee pot going, I couldn't say. Maybe the man stayed with us; perhaps we called him a taxi. There might have been others sleeping behind the sofa or halfway in the closet; I couldn't remember.

Okay, I thought, *I am ready. See you sometime. Maybe in the caves with flame at our back, maybe never.*

I walked for a while. The town was quiet, except for the tourist bar, pumping music, even though few people were inside. Usually on walks, I went up into the rocks, but I was nervous to cross through the adjoining fields at night for fear of stepping on crop rows or startling anyone, so I made a few short loops through town, until I was back at the phone booth again, dialing my parents.

"I have a mobile phone now," I said to their answering machine, and recited the number. I assumed Julian had shared the number to the boardinghouse, but I didn't know. I explained to them how to make an international call, because I was sure they hadn't done it, and I suggested they get a calling card.

"Please call me back," I said. "I'd like to talk to Anne."

That night I dreamed of Daniel in the fire times, the deep smell of sweat and burnt fowl. As always, we made for the caves, tracking along the narrow cow path. I held Anne's hand so tightly she complained, so when there was one moment for breath, I knelt so she could climb to my shoulders. Then, with her head high, she was our lookout, spotting obstacles ahead, screaming *Left!! Left!!* or alerting us to a sharp outcropping—the ruminants, the bovine and the deer family, especially, for all their weight had to be careful on their slender legs—her child's voice ringing above the clatter of hoof and wing. Passing a cache of molting rattlesnakes, she called to them to come down from their hot rocks, to leave their skin.

"We need the sun," one hissed.

"The big ones will keep you warm," she said, and then warned, "Stay back from the small kind."

Still, the king snake eyed one of the prairie dogs, and Anne whipped him with a switch.

"I mean it," she called, and smacked him again.

Our traveling ark, with a girl at its helm.

We were winded, a female ox let us ride her, Anne perched front and me clasping her waist, my seat on the haunches. My daughter was handy with the switch, pushing the cows to the front of the pack, snapping at the rattlers whenever they got ideas.

I scanned for Daniel but didn't see him. I worried that he had fallen behind, and Anne turned to me with the green eyes, the eyes of the girl that had belonged to him and me, who had left us early. I touched her forehead.

We crashed around a bend, and she blinked. Her eyes shifted back to blue.

Anne whipped the ox, and the ox lunged forward, but stumbled some, looking for the other half of her pair. The bull was close though, almost at her side.

When we reached the caves, the reptiles among us curled into the sweating bellies of the beasts, taking their heat, like they had been told they could. Anne looked tired, and I combed her hair with my fingers, picking out burrs and working through knots.

I worried about water, which we all needed, and I worried about the relationship of predator to prey when dawn came.

I watched them, but Anne was watching closer.

"Where's Daniel?" I asked her.

"Who?" she said. Her face was alert. She was scratching a bobcat, calming it with her fingers around its ears.

"Daniel," I said. "He was with us."

She shook her head, shrugged, eyes sapphire, feral. "I don't know that one." She still had the switch in her hand.

"Never mind," I said, and I stood up, to search for water.

When I woke, there was still the sound of heavy breathing all around and the damp, close smells of the animals, but by the time I opened my eyes to the clean, low ceiling, the cave dissolved in the bright, early light.

•

As we did our evening things, Yasemin liked to talk about the village gossip and other items—the past, the price of wheat flour.

And I liked hearing her—her voice was soothing and even, like the way listening to the steady tone of a metronome can be more relaxing than the music following it.

When I came back from Ankara, she was tense. She had let me take the time off because we had no reservations, and that meant money was getting even tighter again—we had celebrated my first paycheck at the hammam and a second without ceremony, and already the stream of guests had dried up again.

"Did you have *anyone*?" I asked her. We were sitting in the kitchen.

"Onur from the carpet shop came for dinner," she said.

"Onur," I said. I couldn't say his name right, with a softness on the *r*. Nearly every Turkish name was like learning a new word. Some names were an actual new word—a woman's name Hava, was the same word as *air*. A man's name Yıldırım, meant *lightning*. Anne's name meant mother.

"I am not in love with him anymore," Yasemin said. When I looked at her, I believed her.

Onur. A common name. It meant *honor*.

She looked around the room. "*Çay, canim,*" she said, so I got up to make the tea. Yasemin was my friend, but we had an order. She told me to make the tea, so I made the tea, but she appended her command with *sweetheart*, like she always did with me.

I had gotten very good at making tea. Wash the leaves, and heat them in the double-boiler pot while the water is warming.

I had learned a lot from her already. She had taught me the local beverages, tea of course, and also ayran, yogurt mixed with salt and water. We had been working on Turkish coffee, but I was not good at it.

The last time I had made an attempt, she took one sip and spit it out.

"It is not so bad as I thought," she said.

I accepted this. "Last time you wouldn't even taste it," I said.

"The smell," she said, "was not delicious."

And Turkish coffee, she admitted, was tricky. It's a sophisticated version of what I grew up calling cowboy coffee, where the grounds are boiled directly in the water. Unlike cowboy coffee, there is a special pot and a meticulous process, one that makes a crema any barista would envy. A process that I had clearly not mastered, though I was getting better.

Also from Yasemin, I was learning to see.

To listen.

To accept the slow times, like bread rising or stew stewing. To pay attention to the smallest stitches in the fabric.

Yasemin would have liked my mother. They were alike in the way they saw through things. Yasemin would have also been a good mother—she was hard sometimes, but that wouldn't be the first way I would describe either of them. There was tenderness, too.

It had taken me some time, but finally I had really gotten to the point where Yasemin was my *abla*, my older sister, the formal-familiar. It is a mode that is not specific, grammatically, in English, but it still exists. When a good girlfriend has children, you can be their aunty, even if you share no blood.

Sometimes you share something bigger than blood.

Even though the tea was already cooking, I wanted a stiffer drink than caffeine, but I kept away from the better wine in the cabinet—maybe she didn't care; but I thought it was bad form if there had been no guests over the weekend, and I was already living off of her kindness. I was already a drain on the kitchen cash-box. Instead, I went to my room for a bottle of local red I'd bought off a bearded man in the vegetable market. It wasn't very good, but I poured it into my tea glass because I thought it was pretty that way, and she didn't correct me as long as I washed it out carefully.

We sat for some time; I poured tea, I went to the courtyard to smoke cigarettes, and then I poured more wine, before I was able to name what I was feeling.

Anger.

I was pissed—pissed I hadn't even *tried* to take care of my visa in Ankara; I had no idea what the consequences were. A fine? Deportation? Both? I had registered when I came into the country. If they re-viewed the logs or verified departures, I didn't know. And I was pissed about Paul's friend Mehmet.

So many years of faithfulness to Julian dissolved under the pressure of beer, dim light, and a bad but rowdy band.

But, when his fingers had laced through mine, it was electric.

But, when his body had pressed against mine, the heat was like fire.

His lanky arms, his sour breath.

In the moment I hadn't wanted anything else.

The crack between Julian and I had started as a hairline—a little fissure, a few leaks; it was nothing as dramatic as the time Yasemin and I walked the marketplace and the chains of *nazar* crashed—bad luck isn't always so obvious—and now I'd made a chasm.

A good marriage can weather much: infidelity and job loss, problem children and empty bank accounts.

I wondered if we had one of these.

Right after I'd moved in with Julian, I had missed my small, solitary apartment—the quiet of it, and the closeness of the walls like a cocoon keeping me safe and contained; like being a child, with the space of the world knit into a few rooms.

I loved Julian then, in the way that fills a person. Being close to him meant being sure.

Sometimes I remembered him, the way we were. We had parties, we had sex on the living room floor and in the kitchen. There were times when he cooked elaborate meals and I would get angry with him, all those dishes. *Ruining Christmas*, I would tell him, *with a pile of pans*, but really, I was smitten, and I couldn't imagine being anywhere else than in an apartment with clacking radiators and pitted hardwood floors and our friends who had nowhere better to be—we took in everyone, from our true companions who didn't want to travel over the holidays to strangers who stopped by because they saw people smoking on the porch. We kept people until morning sometimes, handing out coffee in keg cups or old margarine containers because the mugs had been used the night before, waiting for the sun to pitch its way across the horizon.

Sometimes the light seemed cool and soft, and sometimes brutal.

What I missed about Julian was the moments when I couldn't imagine being anywhere else but with him, the way his hair glowed yellow and his eyes always opened with a shine, a shine for me.

I might have been sighing again.

Yasemin had a tea cup and a little wine I'd poured for her, and she swirled each, the wine a little leggy and the tea thin, and looked up at me. "If you could make Turkish coffee, I would read your fortune."

"I think I know my fortune," I told her.

"*Evet*," she said. *Yes.* "I believe it."

I wasn't sure if she meant she believed I knew or if she believed my fate. I didn't ask.

Between Julian and me there was the obvious, the most ordinary and common kind of discontent. Caught in the loop of working and childrearing and keeping up appearances, real life breaks down.

Sometimes I would close my eyes and think very hard on him. I would remember when we laced hands in a bar, what felt like a hundred years ago. A stranger, who pushed his body into mine, who became a lover, a husband, the father of our child.

In springtime, after we had moved out of our last bad apartment and into our house on Jackson, Julian would head to the back yard and run all the dead winter branches and clumps of dead ferns through a wood chipper he had bought. Sometimes, I watched him from the kitchen window, because I didn't like being outside with the noise. Even after years at a desk job, his palms were still tough. He never wore gloves, and I wasn't sure if that was stupid or sexy.

The wood would churn through and spit onto our compost pile, and I could only think about the grinding of every day, or about nothing. Julian would turn the compost with a shovel, and the compost would steam on cold days. We spread it across the garden, and by the next fall, he would be out chipping again, shredding the stalks from the burnt summer garden and grating leaves.

Sometimes I would catch him pissing on the pile, and I would ask him not to do it, and he would tell me that the addition of healthy urine to compost was actually good.

"It brings up the temperature and kills seeds and spores," he said to me once.

"I don't like it," I said.

In fact, I didn't care so much about the pee. Growing up, my parents used to spread pure farm manure through the yard and the garden; the job may reek a little, but the tomatoes were luscious and the grass blossomed green even through July. Country people don't worry so much about excrement, especially the tame urine of a geologist.

What I didn't like was his stance. I didn't like what seemed like territorialism, like claiming.

There had been things about our life that I enjoyed—I hadn't left my husband and our daughter because of how he handled the compost—there were things that gave me deep comfort. Even when I was frustrated with his matter-of-factness, Julian had steadied me when I needed steadying. When Anne came, there were moments when his calm was saving.

I had heard people say that glass, even though it seems brittle and solid, is actually viscous, and that in the windows of old homes the bottom of the pane will be thicker because gravity pulls it downward. Yet, Julian told me that glass does not really flow. Old windows were made by artisans who cut the plates to fit the casements. The edges of old spun glass are thicker because of chemistry and the human touch—even new glass is thicker at the place of the pour. When it was installed, the thinnest parts would be placed at the top so that the lower edge, where water was more likely to pool, would have the best seal.

Julian had a deep dislike for things like this. It would be maddening to him that people paid so much attention to anecdotes. *If you looked more closely you'd probably see some windows with the thick side up, he had said, from bad installations.* He was sure on this point. *Before I change what I know about silica I would always check for human error.*

Okay, I thought. One of the differences between Julian and me was that I did not care about the tetrahedral structure of anything. One thing that might have been the same between us was that we both liked the idea of the earth doing its slow work of pulling everything back to the dirt.

The fewer things that were absolutely fixed, the happier I was.

Not long after this conversation, Anne accidentally broke a side window. She'd been trying to help me, and I asked her to take the broom back to the closet. The broom itself was taller than she was, and she held it like a lance and pierced the old pane which shattered half of it, and the other half hung, jagged, in the old casement.

I ran to her and swooped her up to protect her sock feet, and then deposited her in the hallway.

"Go put your shoes on, please," I said. She looked concerned, and I felt a twinge at never being able to convince her that I didn't care really when she broke things, because it happens. In life there would be more sharp fragments than she could even imagine.

As she ran off to her room, I collected the fallen broom, and swept the shards into the bin, and I put on my kitchen gloves and broke out the rest of the window. It made a satisfying crunching sound.

"Can I do it?" Anne asked. She was wearing her snow boots.

"I'm worried about your fingers," I said.

"I'll be careful," she said, so I let her put on the gloves, and we wrapped her hands in a kitchen towel for extra measure, and she punched gently through the largest remaining piece, while I cringed; I knew this sound—throwing rocks at windows, breaking bottles against a stone, heaving a drinking glass to the countertop—and how it could both dissolve or amplify a feeling. It seemed to make her less upset, so I was happy, but I still watched carefully for sharp pieces.

After we'd gotten as much out as was practical, I put duct tape around the edges of the frame, where there were still a few jags of window. We swept the floor again, and I asked Anne to get down close to the hardwoods and angle her face to see if she saw any sparkling bits. She found several and presented them to me with her palm upturned, like jewels.

We cut a piece of cardboard and she held it for me as I taped it over the hole.

"It's ugly," she said, so we pulled it out and got her craft box and picked out some decorations—three old buttons, an oversized Christmas bow, and nearly half a jug of gold glitter were secured to the cutout before we put it back up.

The glue that affixed the glitter was drying nicely when Julian came home.

"What happened?" he asked.

"Shoes! Keep your shoes on!" Anne said.

"Jousting," I said. "The window lost."

I saw it in his face—that of course the window broke; it was not liquid, it was not crystalline, it was brittle.

What he didn't see was the sun setting outside the opposite window, streaming orange across the living room. The light caught the glitter and turned our patch job into a kaleidoscope.

Anne saw it.

I saw it.

And Julian went to the closet and got a mop, to make sure we'd gotten every speck.

CHAPTER FIVE

I continued to be surprised that nothing had really moved in me—I got maybe a ripple here and a ripple there, but I couldn't help but think that what I really wanted was a wave. Living in Seattle, I'd seen how the ocean rolls and sputters, but it cleans up after itself. I hadn't.

Yasemin and I were always working, even when we didn't need to be. She had standards I hadn't seen anywhere, that I hadn't even kept in my own home—if a room stayed open, she sent me to wash the walls, clean the p-traps, and polish the stone floors underneath the beds. If the rooms had been slept in, she was particular that I scour carefully for hair. She said there was nothing that felt more unclean than someone else's hair. I hadn't ever thought of it this way, but I agreed with her.

A few weeks had passed, and I absentmindedly wondered about Mehmet, in Ankara, but I didn't really think of him. It was a mistake, and a mistake for me to have gone there, I decided, and since he hadn't contacted me, and I hadn't heard from Paul either, I figured they thought the same.

I wished I had sent Anne a postcard from the capital city, something a little different.

I thought of putting together a package for her, perhaps a belly dancing costume and a box of Turkish Delight. I guess I didn't have much else to tempt her with, beyond bangles and sugar. The postcards to Anne were like listening to half of a conversation. I'd given my address for a reply, but still, not a whisper.

I hope your summer vacation...

I remember when you were very small...

I miss you, I miss you, I hope you understand...

Maybe Julian had been holding my messages, and maybe my mother was now, too. I might have, if it were me. She was so young, not even double digits. I had started sending identical cards to each address, to increase my odds.

The consistency of the chores was like erasing a pencil mark on paper and keeping up the motion long after the mark had vanished and the surface beneath the paper showed through.

This washing, scrubbing, tearing: I couldn't turn it into the wash of foam and salt I wanted. I waited for the break. I tidied up after other people, or I tidied up after no one. I stripped sheets that had been lain in once, I fluffed pillows that no head had touched, I washing and dried and ironed curtains that hadn't even been peeked through. What of the linens on my own bed, in America? I imagined the side that I slept on stayed empty. In the years that I had slept there, I had noticed that the weight of my body had made a divot in the mattress.

Now it must feel sunken, like a grave.

•

Yasemin walked quickly, to everywhere. She was a not a hurried woman, but efficient. She was right handed, but it seemed like she always had something in her left as well. It reminded me of working in the fruit sheds as a kid. In rural Washington anyone who could prove they were at least fourteen could get a job packing fruit. In summers, those of us who weren't already tied up in a family orchard sat the long hours on hard stools, separating the good cherries and apples and pears from the bad. A line boss would walk among us and remind us to use both hands while we sorted; the largest and best fruit went up on a belt above our heads, the bad fruit down a cull shoot, and the average rest of it rolled on by in an endless loop.

These were long days. The only way the money was even close to worth it was the overtime, when the belt would be cruising for ten or twelve hours. The lines were cold, even in the dead heat of summer, but not as cold as the storage coolers, where the guys would come out, wearing long-johns and a stocking cap, frost around their unshaved faces. Everything smelled of bleach, because the fruit rode first in chlorinated water to kill the bugs and the fungus, and then through a perforated chute to dry.

As teenagers, sometimes our parents let us camp in the park by the lake just at the Canadian border, by one of the larger sheds—we were earning money, it was hard for them to say no, and then to ask us to drive or hitch rides with barely-sixteen-year-old friends, already dangerous on the roads, after very long days—and we'd stay up late, smoking someone's bad pot or sharing a stolen bottle of gin, laughing and making very unsophisticated bids toward other tents, but when we closed our eyes, finally, we all dreamed the same dreams of an abundance of fruit, pooling endlessly from the beginning to the end of the line.

I think Yasemin understood I knew something, if not as much as she did, about work, and I think she knew I liked her fast sounds, and that I could track her by her sounds of clatter—her slippers on the tiles, her fingers arranging things in their place. She created order from something as simple as three jugs of olive oil, lined up neatly on the shelf.

She had picked me from the cull pile, given me shelter and work. Out of kindness, and recognition, maybe.

On a slow night, she said, "Yeah, Onur is going to come for dinner again. You should meet him."

I didn't want to, really. I knew him by sight, and I was curious about him, certainly, but there was something ugly between them, and it still felt close to me.

Her cleaning picked up the pace.

I was distracted—I wondered why Julian had stopped answering, even though I knew why. It wasn't like my mother to be so silent; I'd even started saying to her and my dad and maybe my daughter, *I'll call back at 7:15 a.m. your time or I'll call back at 5:30, since I am assuming dinner is still around 6:00,* but the phone rang into dead air.

I was distracted too, about my visa. I wondered if there could be some kind of legal action, and I wondered what Julian would say.

It felt like there was a swirl, a whirlpool, and since Ankara everything was quiet. The excitement of dancing and temporary men had dulled, just like I knew it would, and in just a few days of only me and Yasemin—again—at the chores, I was overwhelmed once more.

I dialed Richard in Bismarck, nothing.

I dialed Michael in Fayetteville, nothing.

I dialed my parents and left more messages. I called them back and left messages specifically for Anne. I stabbed the numbers of my own home and left a message for Anne there as well, since I wasn't sure exactly where she was.

Yasemin eyed me on my trips back and forth from the phone booth, where I was swiping Julian's credit card furiously, my worries about timestamps and being frugal vanished. He wouldn't come for me, I knew it. I was pretty sure he wouldn't turn off the card.

"Make the rice," she told me, lifting an eyebrow, and I washed the grains to a polish while I boiled water.

My glasses fogged as the pot came up to temperature, but I kept my face near the heat—it felt good.

She had told me, only a few weeks in, when we went to the top of Mount Erciyes, to be careful. I was not being careful. I pulled my head away and let my lenses clear and leaned against the counter, pulling a cigarette from my pocket.

"Open the window," Yasemin said, so I did. She didn't like smoking in the kitchen, but she helped herself from my pack.

"Mother*fucker*," I said, trying not to cry.

She exhaled deeply. "I think I know this word," she said. She took another drag and blew smoke through the condensation and steam of the kitchen, as thick as the hammam.

"Is this about your Paul?" she asked.

"He's not mine," I said.

"I know it," she said. "I know this feeling." She stabbed her cigarette out in the sink and crossed the kitchen to open the window a little bit wider. Her hair was wrapped, as always, and her face was slick with sweat.

"Hey," I said. "I can finish dinner."

She nodded. "Okay," she said, and went to her room to change.

I didn't know what I was feeling, so I focused, the way Yasemin had taught me to focus. I finished the rice and set the table, smoothing every wrinkle of the cloth. It was my job to scrub the table linens free of dropped food and wipes of oily fingerprints, working at the spots with a lemon, and hanging them in the sun to bleach, and I was glad that I could not find any spots. I arranged the food, taking care to wipe the rims of the serving containers and polish the water spots off of the cutlery.

Maybe I could go home, I thought. Maybe I should.

When Onur arrived, he was as immaculate as my table, in a pressed shirt and trousers, only a suggestion of dust on his shoes from the short walk. Yasemin, too, came from her room and she looked pretty in a purple scarf and emerald dress; she'd washed her face and lined her eyes. They kissed in greeting, two quick pecks on either side of the cheeks. I was embarrassed, some, that I hadn't made time to change, still in a dusty skirt and ragged top.

We sat at the guest table for dinner, where there was space for twelve. Yasemin at one head, Onur and I on either side of her, a long empty plank extending to the other side of the room. We served ourselves, and I noted how ragged my cuticles were when compared to the polished spoons.

It was hard to make conversation between us three, with so many secrets. The overhead light was burning, and the candles were lit.

Sometimes I would catch Onur looking at me, and sometimes, I would look at him and I would catch him looking away, and I wished someone would come into the small lobby, and I wished it would be Paul. I thought back to when we had taken our trip up the mountainside, when the snow started, when Yasemin saved us, and how I'd put my sock foot on top of his when we were drying out in a café. It was only two people touching each other, through cloth, but now he was my friend.

To be sure, I had been curious about Onur, but it felt complicated to be so close to him. He and Yasemin spoke in English, as a courtesy, but I felt like a child waiting to be excused, and the meal was very long. Yasemin glowed, but my face felt greasy and my glasses were smudged in a way that I knew would need more than just a wipe on my shirt.

We ate through several long silences, punctuated only by compliments from Onur and thanks from Yasemin. I wanted a drink and a cigarette and I'd moved

beyond being a child to a teen, where I willed my phone
to ring.

"I can make coffee," I said, but Yasemin gave me
a look.

"I'll make coffee," she said.

"Maybe we go outside," Onur suggested. "It's
nice." June had not gotten hot.

"Go," she said to us. "I'll come."

I tried to help clear the table, but she waved me
off, and it wasn't until then that I understood she was
just as uncomfortable as I was, looking for a reprieve in
the kitchen and the work. I wondered sometimes if she
missed her school life, when she'd studied chemistry in a
white coat with her unbound hair skimming her waist,
and I thought that she probably did, even though she
had been choosing something different for a very long
time.

Paul had not come through the door, and for a
moment, as I led Onur to the courtyard, I thought I
could resolve myself. I could forget about one toe
stacked on top of another. I could forget about Ankara
and the voting booth ink on my hip, and maybe I could
forget why I'd left in the first place: my dreams of fire
and everyday things that pushed me from Julian. He'd
grabbed my hand once, and there was a lot of space
between that place and here.

My ring finger was bare, but I had on a silver
bracelet from home.

There were outside lights, but I hadn't switched
them on, and I apologized and made the turn to go back
inside, but Onur waved me back. He lit a cigarette, and

he offered me one, and I took it. Inside I heard a pan crash; Yasemin making a first attack at the dishes.

Still, we didn't have much to say, but it was easier in the dark. We smoked quietly, and Yasemin joined us eventually with a tray of expertly made coffee and perfect tiny pastries.

We stayed up late, in the cool night air, sometimes talking and sometimes not.

•

The next day was Friday. The call for prayer came every day, seven times, but Friday was the holy day and more of the faithful heeded it. I liked the rhythm of Islam, like the rhythm of our chores. I was not allowed to forget—always the breaking of a holy voice against the dry Anatolian air, always the splash of a scrub brush into a bucket.

The call to prayer punctuated our daily lives, and even if I had stopped being so moved by it every time, I think Yasemin and I both felt frequently prostrate. I cannot say that I was prostrate to *Allah*, but I felt closer to the idea of faith than I ever had, as the notes of the call scattered through the sky.

That morning, I trudged to the phone booth. My head was foggy. As the night had worn on with Yasemin and Onur, we'd opened wine, and I was paying for it. I counted out what time it would be in Pacific America, 11 p.m.

It was a ritual: call my mother, my husband, and hope for my daughter.

The Pull of It

I wandered in the town square some, nodding at the vendors who knew me, looking away from the tourists who recognized me as American. I thought if I were better, I would talk to them and lead them back to the boardinghouse, but neither Yasemin nor I were good at this. We kept the wanderers who found us by the hand-painted signs—a sign at the bus stop, a sign at Onur's carpet place, a final sign that confirmed arrival— but we didn't prospect in the streets.

The Friday noon prayers would be the busiest, like a Sunday morning, and even though it was still early, I wanted to get back. Yasemin had been sleeping when I left, or at least I hadn't heard her. I went a few blocks out of my way, by Onur's, but even though the shop was open, I didn't see him in his usual place in front, wrangling the tired with his textiles.

I went to my room, and the air was cool. I thought I would lie down for a while, but I slept longer than I wanted, awakened midday by the call to prayer. In the place between dream and light, I heard a wet thud, like a tennis ball against a garage door, the sound when something soft smashes onto something hard. It took me a moment to calibrate, to negotiate the space between sleep and awake, but I knew, when my eyes had opened all the way, that the sound I'd heard was not a dream.

It took me a second to find my sandals, and then I sprinted toward the sound, finding Yasemin in the courtyard, on the stairs, head against the ground, feet reaching up to the fourth and fifth steps. There was red soaking her hair where her scarf had come loose.

180

Later I thought it was stupid, in a medical crisis, but the first thing I thought to do was to pull her skirt to a more proper length. It had come up around her waist, and I moved it gently to cover her knees.

I tried to wake her. She would not budge.

At first I thought I shouldn't move her, and then I thought since her head was bleeding it should be elevated. I wasn't sure, so I half-lifted her—she felt so light—so I could reposition her against the stairs.

Propped up, there was no movement in her eyes; her breath was very shallow.

"Yasemin," I said to her.

I then ran, with the energy one has when they don't know where they are going but know they must get there fast.

I stopped at the carpet shop. Onur was outside, and he must have seen me coming down the narrow, dusty street. We raced back, Onur leading. He was tall and swift. I was only a few seconds behind him, but by the time I got there he had called for help from his mobile phone. He was holding her in his arms and there was blood on his vest.

It was like the dreams of fire, of getting to safety in the caves—heat and the tumbling of feet not moving fast enough.

As soon as the medics came, we ran back to the carpet shop so Onur could pull out his car, and we could follow the ambulance to Kayseri. The trunk of the car was dented to the point where it was almost caved in. I realized I didn't even know the number for Turkish 911; I asked Onur about the Turkish emergency line, and he showed me the last digits dialed from his phone: 112.

He smelled like cigarettes and sweat and wool and something sour. Fear, maybe.

The drive seemed very long. There was no radio, just a hole in the dash.

I wanted to say something to him, but I wasn't sure what I had to say. We rode with our silence and the scream of the ambulance, Onur's foot heavy on the gas, desperately trying to keep sight of the woman we both loved.

I wished we had stopped that day to bow toward the east. I kept thinking of Yasemin in the moment her feet lost traction on the stairs. The sky was full from the sound ringing from the minarets, but it could not hold her. She sliced the air and was taken by the inevitable pull of gravity, and I wished I were there as she sailed headfirst toward the stones to reach for her hand or to somehow break her fall.

The sun was so bright and my heart was still pounding from running back and forth with Onur. He rammed the accelerator, and when the road curved I grabbed the handle on the passenger side and closed my eyes. I wanted to tell him to wear his seatbelt, and I wondered how it was for him, doing this drive, heading to the same hospital where his wife had probably passed, those years ago in winter.

And here came my wave.

It seemed so clear now Yasemin was my anchor.

We were going so fast, we were right on the bumper of the ambulance, and for a moment I wondered if Onur would pass, but he stayed, there, just a few feet back, until the hospital appeared, and he turned hard and screeched into the parking lot, while the ambulance headed for the emergency doors.

•

We check in, we waited. I worked through it in my head, to stop thinking about the now, the after: she falls, *düşüyor*; she has fallen, *düştüydü*; she fell, *düştü*; she fell from stairs *merdinvenler düştü*.

The doctor could not let Onur nor I see her, because we were not family, and he apologized for this. It was not his rule and it was clear that he did not like it. We had stayed in the waiting room, silently, overnight. It was a public hospital and the major one in the region, so it was busy. I slept for a few hours on the white floor. The tiles were cool through my light clothes. Onur gave me his jacket for a pillow. I wondered if I should call Paul.

There was a strange feeling of commerce in the hospital, as boys came through in blue jackets selling tea and snacks and little packets of tissues. I bought all three with some crumpled lira I'd found jammed in my pocket.

She died the next day, just as the last June light left the sky.

I wanted to say that I could feel the moment that Yasemin slipped to the other side, but it might have only been Onur's hand at the back of my neck, nudging me gently to sit up when he heard the doctor's shoes clicking down the hallway.

I hoped she had gone in peace.
Inşallah.

•

Onur said he would return to the village. We
had walked through the grounds of the hospital to find
a teahouse. We smoked for a while and let our teas grow
cold. Even my earrings felt heavy on my lobes.

He held my arm, and he let me lean into him. I
thought I could see how Yasemin had loved him. He
took my mobile number. We figured out that I would
not return with him directly, but he could find me at
the guesthouse in a day. I wasn't sure what I would do,
exactly, but I couldn't go back. We were empty anyway,
and with no one at home all day, we would not have
reservations. And I couldn't care.

"What will happen now?" I asked him.

"*Bilmiyorum,*" he said. I knew this word, but I
didn't know if he meant he didn't know or he didn't
understand. It could have been both.

"Laura," he said. "I go."

"*Tamam,*" I said. *Okay.*

The waiter came and cleared our glasses, and I
motioned for fresh tea. Onur rose heavily, his curls
flattened on one side, his trousers very wrinkled. I stood
with him, and we kissed on each cheek, in the
customary way.

"*Allah'a ısmarladık,*" Onur said.

"I entrust you to God," I said, repeating it back
to him in English.

184

He nodded, and my eyes were wet again.

We were strangers and I thought we would stay so. I wondered if he would remarry now that Yasemin was gone, and I wondered what I would do.

Maybe she had released us both. I looked at Onur's face. I think he wanted it even less than I did.

•

The hospital at Kayseri was close to the university—just across a parking lot. I knew that Paul lived nearby, but I wasn't sure exactly where. I stayed at the teahouse and drank what seemed like a hundred cups of tea, even though it was the same tepid glass that I couldn't finish. I ran out of cigarettes and I paid my bill, then found a shop and bought more tobacco. I sat on a bench for a while. My hair felt greasy. I thought of Anne. I hadn't felt so empty since she'd emerged from me.

I felt the weight of my phone in my pocket. I still had plenty of battery. No one called me—I had three numbers now: Paul, Yasemin, and Onur. I sent Paul a text message: AT THE HOSPITAL: YASEMIN GONE. SHE FELL.

The reply was immediate. IN KAYSERI? I'M COMING. WAIT BY THE CAMPUS MOSQUE. 10 MINUTES.

He was there in seven.

He was unshowered, but so was I.

"I don't…" I said.

He pulled me to him.

185

"The emergency number is 112," I said. "I didn't know. She fell down the stairs. I should have called, but I didn't know."

"Quiet," he said. "Sshh."

"Onur called," I said. "Onur brought me here. He waited with me."

"Let's go back to my flat," Paul said.

"Is your wife there?" I asked.

"Of course she is," Paul said. "We live there."

"It's 112, Paul," I said. "Fire is 110. Police is 155. I asked him."

"I know," he said.

"I should have called," I said.

"I don't think the dispatch speaks English. You were right to get Onur. Come on," he said.

He took my hand. I wasn't sure I could move my legs.

"Can we sit here for a minute?" I asked.

"Of course," he said.

We sat until the sun started to sink, my head resting on his shoulder.

"I don't know what I am doing," I said to him finally.

"It's okay," he said. "No one does."

•

I liked Paul's wife immensely. She had clearly been waiting for us, as there was food and tea prepared. There were snacks of nuts and dried fruit in tiny dishes on a try, and the flat smelled of mint.

"Hello," I said to her. She was very pretty.

"I am sorry to hear what happened," she said.

Their flat was small and some of Paul's rock sculptures sat on the floor.

His wife carried the tray out to the patio. They had a small portable fire-pit, and she lit it. The embers gave off little heat, but glowed orange in the failing light.

We three sat in a circle and were mostly quiet. I sipped the mint tea.

"You should stay with us tonight, Laura," Paul's wife said. "Or we will ride the bus back with you. You need a jacket. I'll find you one."

It wasn't cold, the first of July, but I was shivering.

When she went inside, I looked at Paul.

"You should come to Istanbul with me. I'm leaving soon," he said.

"She's very kind," I said.

"Of course she is," Paul said. "I wouldn't have married her if she wasn't."

I felt this, and thought of my husband. I missed Anne fiercely, and I wanted to tell Paul about her, but I kept my lips pressed tight.

He had talked about Istanbul the way people talk about Atlantis—with curiosity and reverence and a kind of suspicious awe. He described the shops and cafés and crowds to me over and over again, though he knew I had spent two and a half weeks there upon my arrival in Turkey; but two weeks is nothing in one of the largest cities in the world. At two weeks, it's still hard to negotiate the crowds and the landscape.

"Let's take a walk," he said.

He poked his head inside and said something low to his wife. She scrambled to the sliding glass door and handed over a ragged windbreaker, and I put it on. We set out, crossing the shared lawn of the apartment building they lived in, our feet swishing through the grass that hadn't died or gone dormant. I smelled charcoal burning and heard voices; there were some boys from the university on the far end of the yard barbequing and drinking beer.

The hospital would prepare Yasemin's body in accordance with Islamic tradition; she would be washed from head to toe and buried in clean earth. I hoped this was what she wanted, and I could not imagine that there would be anything else.

We stopped on the steps of a half-finished amphitheater halfway between Paul's apartment and the university. I had heard Paul talk about it, speculating that the financiers would never finish having the concrete poured, and as long as I had known him he hadn't reported much progress on it. The structure now remained a half circle butted up against a wall of dirt.

He produced a flask from his jacket and passed it to me. The taste of whiskey was sweet and dark.

I had told Yasemin once I liked being with Paul, and she had warned me. I did like him. I liked the weight of his hand when he passed me the flask and then let his fingers fall to my knee, I liked his long legs and his gapped teeth, liked his dirty blond hair—the kind of hair that always wants the sun to help show its color.

"I'm sorry about Ankara," I said. "Your friend."

"It doesn't matter," he said. "Come to Istanbul with me."

"And then what?" I asked. I had leaned my head onto his shoulder because it was too hard to hold it up on my own. No one could see us in the dark anyway.

"And then nothing," he said. "And then, who knows." He reached his other arm across his body so that he could cup my face.

I told him I was a woman in hiding. I told him that I had to go back to the boardinghouse first, and see what I could straighten out of Yasemin's affairs. I needed to find out if there would be a public service. I needed to say something—I wasn't sure what—to Onur.

He chuckled a little. "We're all in hiding."

"Not everyone," I said.

"Everyone," he said.

•

It was late before I untangled myself from Paul, and he offered to ride with me, and I refused, but he insisted that he wait with me for the direct bus. We'd drained the flask and I was so tired I could barely stay awake. He gave instructions to the driver of where to let me off if I didn't wake up, handing him a crumpled note. It was only a forty-five minute ride and I slept the entire way.

Stepping out of the bus in the village square was almost like my first time—I felt so tentative and confused. I picked my way through the streets to the boardinghouse, and only the light in my room burned through the orange curtains. I must have left it on.

•

Yasemin's service was simple. Some of the women we had seen in the *hamam* came to pay respects, along with some old village men who I figured had known her father. Onur and I stood shoulder to shoulder through the prayers.

Onur did most of the work in settling the estate. There was still some debt on the boardinghouse, but there were no heirs or remaining family, so the bank would retain the property. They encouraged Onur and me to take anything personal for a remembrance. The rest, like the linens and the pantry, would go to the mosque for distribution.

I had never been in Yasemin's room before. It was tidy and spare. Her clothes hung neatly in a doorless closet. There was a small box of simple jewelry and a framed picture of Onur as a much younger man on the dresser. I hoped he would see it.

Also in a frame was a postcard of the periodic table. I removed it from the glass. It was dated from when Yasemin would have been at university and the postmark was from Ankara. I recognized her handwriting, and even though I couldn't quite understand the note, the greeting to her parents *Anne* and *Baba* was clear enough, as was her looping signature. She'd sent it to them a long time ago, and now it came with me in my blue daypack.

I left the curtains she had made swinging on their rails.

The postcard-sized periodic was all I took from Yasemin's room. Though I would never understand it in the same way she had, I think I did understand something about the order. The alkali, the metalloids, the carbon group. I looked for Y on the table, and there it was, Yttrium, a rare earth mineral. *İtriyum* in Turkish. Yasemin had told me about this one. It could be used to create synthetic garnets.

Named after the seeds of pomegranates, which according to the Koran grow in the gardens of paradise, the garnet is deep red. It is lustrous and smooth, like the flesh of a still heart.

•

He convinced me, finally, Paul.

It hadn't been that long since he had planted the seed of traveling with him to Istanbul, but he had tended it carefully.

Finally, he said, "Come on. It'll distract you from Yasemin."

I felt like he stabbed me, just saying her name.

We were on the telephone. Paul was on his mobile, at the amphitheater. I could hear the echo of concrete. I was staying with Onur, in his spare room. He had said that he didn't think I should remain at the boardinghouse, and I agreed. He said he didn't care about the village gossips. Neither did I. Paul, though, I could tell didn't like it, even though he had no rights to me.

The truth was, I'd been thinking of going to Istanbul too, but for a different reason—the airport. I'd been at the internet café, had even checked my email hoping for some news of Anne, and when my inbox was empty, I'd navigated to an airline site, and started punching in the codes IST to SEA. One way.

I'd kept up the pace of calling and posting, and if this was Julian's plan, to withhold Anne until I came back for her, it was working.

During the day, Onur went to the carpet shop; sometimes I went with him because there was a familiarity in the looping quality of the work. The store was piled high with textiles and heavy with the smell of dust and wool, and when there were no customers, Onur stacked and restacked the rugs, counting them, getting a look at the ones that might be buried at the bottom and making a mental catalog so he would know where to find the right shade of blue or a particular design. I organized the space around the register, swept dust out of corners, thinking of Yasemin, always circling meticulously.

Sometimes I went walking. Always in the evening I cooked for Onur, because I didn't have anything else to do, and the cooking was another way I could remember. Yasemin would be at my shoulder, instructing, approving or disapproving. When we ate, Onur and I were usually silent, looking at our plates.

We missed her.

"Okay," I had said to Paul, "fine." He was right that I needed some distraction. "Are you leaving your wife?" I asked.

"I don't know what I'm doing, Laura."

"I need a day," I said.

"Tomorrow night?" It was Monday. "I'll meet you at the bus stop," he said. "It's twelve hours. We'll take the overnight."

•

When I told Onur it was time for me to leave, he pulled me to him, the first full embrace we'd had, and I felt his chest heaving. It was a long time before he let me go, and then he disappeared into the back of the shop and came back to press a stack of bills into my hand.

"*Hayır*," I said. *No*.

"*Evet*," he said. *Yes*, and he walked away, to show the conversation was finished.

That Tuesday I paced around the carpet shop, not sure what I should say to Onur, but wanting to stay close. In the afternoon, I walked back to Yasemin's for the first time, and it had been boarded. If my curtains were still up, I couldn't tell.

I went to the phone booth and swiped Julian's card. I always wondered if he would turn it off, but the dial pad lit, and I started in on the long strings of numbers that had become a ritual. No one answered, but I left messages for my parents and Julian and for my brother. *I'm leaving here. I'm making my way back. Not sure when. You can call my mobile.*

By evening I had organized my few things in my pack so that it sat small on my back.

When it was time to leave, Onur thanked me for helping him around the shop and in the kitchen.

"Onur," I said. "You are kind."

"*Allah'a ısmarladık*," he said, and kissed me once on both cheeks.

"I entrust you to God," I said, repeating it back to him in English.

This was the way in which he and I had come to say goodbye.

•

Istanbul, after being landlocked for so long.

Now I had only Onur's money and the same blue daypack I'd had when I'd set out six months ago. There was a little jewelry again tangled in the bottom. I wore a necklace and a set of silver rings. My gold wedding band was tucked into a pocket. I had almost wanted to start wearing it again, to remind me of Julian, to have something physical that would start to tether me.

I hoped the postcard of Yasemin's periodic table was staying flat.

At first Paul had been trying to lure me to Istanbul with the promise of American movies and the prospect of pork at a foreign grocery. Now I was with him, trying to get over my friend and figure out how to

Wendy J. Fox

get back on a plane. The visa, again, nagged me. I wasn't sure what would happen.

I'd covered my hair for the bus ride, which wasn't at all necessary. Paul was wearing an oversized Kurdish head wrap—a black-checkered square scarf looped into a mound. He said it helped keep him cool. We didn't look Turkish at all, but we looked less American. I guess we liked to pretend we weren't ourselves, Paul and I, and for a second I wondered what I was doing with him. *Tickets*, I thought, *he is very good at tickets. Have him help you.*

We had a nice day. We got off the bus on the Asian side of the city, mostly for the benefit of the twenty-minute ferry ride to the European continent. And after twelve hours, we were both ready to stand up. I had fond memories of water travel from my childhood, and since then every ferryboat has seemed the same— despite the rust and the barnacles up and down the sides, and the creaky seats, there was the feeling of security, of something very sure. It was the feeling that came from floating; the vessel rested on the water, the wind pushing, the current carrying, the shape of the channel showing where to land, with none of the defiance of flying or recklessness of automobiles.

Paul and I leaned over the bow and watched the water peel away from the hull and smoked cigarettes and bought some tea from the vendor who traversed the length of the rocking ship with his tray of glass and sugar and hot *çay* with the grace of a woman on a tight wire.

195

The salt air blew my scarf loose, and the air was temperate, even for summer.

But as our ferry came up to the docks at Eminönü, I was shocked at the crush of people, and the *traffic*—water traffic, foot traffic, car traffic, train traffic. I had forgotten it. I was from a small town, and yes, I had lived in Seattle, and yes, I had been to Istanbul before, but that was before I'd holed up with Yasemin in central Anatolia, where the distance, the harsh weather, and village life protected us. I think I hadn't known how much small town life agreed with me.

The terminals were built on a narrow strip of pilings and concrete with no proper sidewalk; the foot-traffic boundary on the opposite side of the water was marked by a disastrously busy street.

We walked along the edge of the docks through the shouting; the smoke from the old boats and the fish restaurants butted right up against the seawall, and the bands of tourists were like ducklings waiting for their mother.

I recognized this place. I had sold my clothes here, close to the spice market, where the metro tracks snaked, along with the flocks of pigeons and little boys with their jars of shoe polish, and the perpetually unemployed men in their sagging pants packing their fishing poles to the Galata bridge.

Thank you, I mouthed to Paul when he pushed me onto our bus, paying both our fares and shoving me into the window side of the dual seats. The coach filled quickly. Paul gave up his seat for an older, covered woman, as is the custom in the villages. I smiled at him for this. He was acting a little bit country; I always did.

The covered woman gave me a nod of approval—she was pleased with Paul as well, and then she tugged the top of my scarf a little to cover where my bangs had slipped out after being hauled halfway across the country and then through Eminönü.

Paul thought it would be easy to find a little boardinghouse for the night, so we did not worry about our lodgings immediately. He had warned me to pack light. I had shrugged. I didn't have anything to pack heavy with, having made this kind of exit before. I think maybe he didn't know just how little I needed—and I'd gotten very used to the village custom of picking out a set of clothes and wearing the same all week long. Doing laundry by hand will do that to you.

Did I hear bells? Did I see stars? Did the flag flutter down to the grass?

It was late morning. Paul wanted a movie. There were two movies that changed every other week in Kayseri, and sometimes the pictures filmed in English were dubbed. In Göreme, there was not even a cinema.

It is funny how even in the twenty-first century, the sparkle of a city can get through like that. The way a movie house will pull you in. How there are always apples to be picked.

We ducked into a theatre on İstiklāl Caddesi, the central street in the old town, and the heart of cultural life. Paul explained to me the custom of tipping—something not practiced in the small towns, and I watched how deftly he slipped the note into the usher's hand, and how the usher held the bill there, between his palm and his long flashlight.

Time was slow for me. I leaned into Paul's shoulder. Once on top of Mount Erciyes I had put my sock foot on top of his; now I slipped my arm through his arm. Once in an unfinished amphitheater he had wrapped his arms around me. I didn't hold his hand, though I wanted to. Sometimes he would tip his head down and rest his cheek on my hair, and sometimes he would kiss my temple very lightly. Or maybe he didn't kiss me. Maybe I only wanted that. I tried to understand how I could go back. How I should.

We kept our eyes fixed on the screen, captivated, and in the dark, I uncovered my head.

I knew the smell of his clothing, the Alo! detergent and the faint smell of his flat—dust and cooking oil and steam from the central heat and parsley and beer.

I remember what we watched, but it didn't matter. What mattered was later, when we came out of the theater, and we blinked in the afternoon sun and went off in search of a drink. In Kayseri or Göreme we would walk to the *tekel* and change in our empty bottles of Efes beer for fresh ones. I had not always liked beer, but I came to enjoy the amber taste of the government-brewed hops. I liked the way my fingers felt around the thick bottles, slick with condensation, my mouth and Paul's mouth touching the same shape.

So, still blinking after the dark of the theatre, still flushed with feeling his arm laced through mine, I smiled so wide and I said to him that we were in the city now. We had some choices.

He laughed, and he looked away. He was positively shining. He'd taken off his wrap and had it draped over one arm.

He stopped at a stand and bought another pack of cigarettes and lit one. The vendor was out of small coin and gave him his change in chewing gum.

"Let's walk," I said. I put my arm into his again.

"Okay," he said.

I was getting very hungry. "Do you want to eat?" I asked him. "We probably don't even have to eat Turkish food."

"Laura," he said, "you love Turkish food."

I looked at him. He smoked. His eyes were hazel and very clear.

He reached for my head and pushed off my scarf. "You don't have to wear that," he said.

"I know," I said.

I loved to be like this with men, with my shoulder just slightly leaning into their shoulder. The late summer sun was full on my face, and I pushed just a little on Paul so I could feel him push back. I looked at the side of his head—he was handsome in a very American way. He was newly wearing a goatee on his strong chin. Moving down the street was slow going, as we picked our way around the garbage sweepers and shopkeepers in their doorways and groups stopped to chat and the constant influx of shoppers and walkers and tourists streaming in from the side streets and the trolley slowly coming up the gentle incline.

The light was just starting to lean toward afternoon. I was really getting very hungry, but hunger is just another ache, I had learned, another hole to fill up, so I swallowed hard and Paul and I kept walking. I was beaming at him, I am sure. I felt it. Like light or a smiling child. I was wondering, as we passed a travel agency, if I should talk to him about going. If I should ask him to help me.

He was quiet.

In contrast to him, an American might be able to tell our differences. He, the Californian, with that particular slope of body, constantly reaching for the sun like a heliotrope; I, from the northern edges of Washington, pale and freckled and thick through the middle.

I looked at Paul again. His shoulder was warm and he seemed taller. Like his head was farther away.

His face had turned down a little. And it also seemed, though we were not so far into the afternoon, that the sun was falling fast, but like some other coastal places, it was mild in Istanbul. We kept walking along through the crowds. My arm still in his.

I smelled the exhaust of the open cook fires at the *kebap* restaurants and from the huge racks of rotating lamb at the cafeteria-style eateries. When I had been in Istanbul touristing, before I'd hopped on a bus heading east, I loved to get *dürüm*, a piece of flatbread rolled around chunks of beef and lamb from the upright spits and stuffed with vegetables. Young Turks covered their *dürüm* in ketchup and mayonnaise and sprinkled salt on between bites. I liked ketchup and mayonnaise as well, but what I liked better was sitting in the back of a little ramshackle shop or standing out on the street with my food, eating it down until there was nothing but greasy paper left. I watched how Turkish people would swipe the wrapper across their mouths and hands before they tossed it into the bin. In the shops, there was always lemon cologne near the change box, and it was splashed liberally across the face and hands.

On the street, I'd wipe my fingers across the leg of my pants and call it good.

I was not really okay, when my feet had first touched ground on the European side of the city. Returning, albeit with Paul, reminded me of those first moments of choosing exile from America, while wandering through the streets whose names I could hardly pronounce, tripping on the cobbled stones and my own loose shoes.

The everyday is strange. It's more than just the inevitable way that newness wears off, it's more of a complacency, or an acceptance—like the way no one can smell their own smells quite so strongly. So we spend all this time: we build the marriage, we paint the house, we birth the children, but it's nothing but fixture, a prettier hanger on a prettier rail against a prettier shade of paint on which to hang the same old tired blouse.

In my first weeks, I paid attention because I *had* to find my way. The street signs were blue and not green. The alphabet had more letters. The ordinary shops were textured in a way I could not have expected—barbers like mid-century America, teahouses packed with men like I had never seen, and for all the macho culture, affection: men holding hands; men kissing each other's cheeks; men with their fingers in another man's hair, playing dominoes and dice.

Early on, I was pulled by the typical Eastern things Westerners are drawn to, like spice markets and jangling dance costumes, but it was the ordinary that held me. Boys no older than nine or ten shining shoes in the street or selling packets of tissues, and girls collecting trash and begging with their mothers, and the flash of metal—like a fishing lure, like a welder's spark—at the gold markets.

Before I intentionally missed my flight, I knew how Julian would feel—*how could she do this to her daughter?* And underneath genuine concern for our girl was: *how could she do this to me?* I couldn't say that I would react differently, if it were me, but then again, he would never, ever do something like run off. We were not the same.

Paul had been quiet. My stride hit with his; I kept my arm linked in his. I wished then that I knew more about him, more about what he had left.

We didn't have many taboos, Paul and I, but if there was one, America was it.

I knew his father worked in a tire shop, and he knew I had been in the northwest. Beyond that, we didn't talk about the place much. I had mentioned my brothers once but hadn't even hinted at Anne. Maybe it was important in this place to speak and live and exist in the present. Anatolia had enough history to go around, anyway.

That's when I stopped to stare in a shop window. It was the dusk prayer, and while I could pick out the sound of *ezan* through the traffic and the calls of vendors and the low whine of the fourteen million residents of Istanbul breathing and talking and just being, it was nothing like Kayseri or even Göreme where it came like the sirens for tsunami warnings I was used to in Washington. I could hear the first few beats, and then the echo, and then the beginning of the next pulse at the next towering minaret.

Paul and I had entered into a more upscale shopping district, and there, like a kaleidoscope or a handful of beads, behind the glass was layer after layer of color—shoes stacked like a display of decorated sweets.

I uncoupled my arm with his for just a second, and I got closer to the glass. It was the way the display bloomed that pulled me in.

There were bright silk shoes and dyed leather shoes, beaded shoes and shoes that laced up with ribbon. A ballroom shoe the color of mica. Black flats as glossy as fresh lipstick.

It had been a long time since I had spent much time wearing anything other than the practical, but I still enjoyed the architecture of shoes, the way they allowed the wearer to toggle her height or the slope of her leg, the reshaping of the foot.

And it was thrilling to be away from where everything came in the same brown and muted yellows of the surrounding landscape, fashion as exciting as dirt.

In the shop window, some of the shoes rested on tiny shelves spaced along the wall, and others paved the display box's floor or were suspended from the ceiling.

"Paul," I said, turning partway, "this is incredible." The craftsmanship was remarkable even to someone who didn't love slippers, boots and pumps. Each shoe reminded me of the prize behind the doors of an advent calendar, delicate and painted as carefully as miniatures.

"Come here," I said, and waved my hand at him.

He was pacing a little, smoking. I could see his entire head—he was looking right at me and I could also see the back of his hair reflected in the window on the opposite side of the narrow street.

"Paul!" I called at him. "Come *here!*"

When I turned again, he hadn't moved. The crowd on the pedestrian-only section of this street was thick, but I could tell his eyes were fixed on me.

Why won't he come, I thought.

I gave him another look—he was half staring up at the sky, half toeing the cobbles—and turned back to the window. He was like this sometimes. He'd get distant and stand off.

Without Paul to share my excitement and his arm to keep me warm, the charm of the window started to wane. I gave a final study to the buckles on a single Mary Jane, and walked half out into the street, hoping he was finally as hungry as I was.

Paul, though, was gone.

I went back to the window. *Try again!* I picked a different shoe, this one a grape Sabrina heel with a band of sequins around the opening for the big toe.

I took in the display for a few more moments, and turned to go.

But when I went to the place I had last seen him, he was still gone.

I looked for his scarf, the top of his blond head.

He had sifted into the crowd, like water into dry ground.

And I stood in that exact spot until I was out of cigarettes, until the light failed, until I was past any kind of doubt that he'd just stepped into an alley to look at something or decided he needed a minute to himself.

The stores were beginning to close and my legs were cramped and my fingers cold.

I understood. Me, of all people.

I knew he had not taken me to Istanbul for the express purpose of leaving me in the street, and I thought back to how this city had seduced me, and I'd skipped my flight back to America and boarded a bus.

If there was guilt involved, I was just as guilty, even if by association, or by implicit understanding.

Paul, I thought again. *So you needed to go.*

I might have gone with you.

I wanted to go with you.

I miss you already.

The sun had gone down, and it was the middle of July and the light had faded fast. I was cold. There was wind off the Bosporus like empty gray air.

I went looking for a teahouse that would be okay for a foreign woman—most, really, are, but there are some where the chairs are packed with smoking, *rakı*-drunk men who've been hypnotized by the sound of dominoes and dice tumbling across the tables—not dangerous, but the doors are also not open.

I thought of taking the bus back to Kayseri. I thought I might know how to take the train at least partway to the bus station, and I had enough money for a car, if not. I thought of calling Onur. I debated this after ducking into a small, yellow-lit shop where I drank my tea. It was late enough that I was not really comfort-table alone, but I reminded myself I was in the city, on the coast, not in an inland village. Out of central Anatolia, I realized I was also not as relatively tall, as I had gotten used to being, and I was not as obvious, certainly not so obviously Western. It was true I had been in hiding with Yasemin, but I was anything but anonymous.

I was like trying to hide black paint under a coat of white.

I finished my tea. I had another, along with a pastry. I used the toilet, and I paid with Onur's money. I left the café, I went back into the street, and turned again down İstiklâl Caddesi. Still, I had not decided what to do. Not sure I could face the twelve hours on the bus alone, I thought to look for a hotel, and I stepped into a side street. Clearly, I could see the red, vertical neon sign on my right spelling out *Marko Paşa*, and beyond that, another vertical sign that I thought read *Residence*, and between on my left, the Hotel Çağ.

I know that I did not make it inside any of these places.

I heard a man's voice say, *Natasha?*

And I said, *Hayır*. No. *Nein*. Even a bumpkin knew—fair or unfair—that Natasha was the catchall name for a foreign sex worker.

He said, "Lady, I pay you 300 Euros."

I looked at the man. He was medium build, but I could see even in the dark that he, like me, was not local. I could not identify the accent.

"No," I said.

Usually, even in a dark alley, even in an unfamiliar country, even in the company of idle, half-drunken men, people will do you a kindness. I believed this. I *had* to believe this. I still believe this, but people get angry when they are refused.

I had lived long enough to have a few scary, late-night encounters. By the back side of puberty, most women have. Whether it was reckless or savvy, I'd always managed to take a side step before anything terrible happened.

But that night, missing Paul and Yasemin and even Onur the way I would miss breathing, I may have been ready for the sadness to take me.

My bones hurt.

My head was like someone wrapped my thinking parts in gauze.

I was having trouble keeping my eyes from floating off.

I tried to return to the main street. I wanted to run, but like a dream, my legs barely moved.

Already they were at my back, already my face on the pavements, already the taste of a stranger's fingers across my mouth.

•

The Pull of It

When I woke up, there were bruises across my thighs, like suddenly I'd become a plum, a starburst of raspberry at my eye. A broken pinky. A licorice whip welt down my shoulder like an arrow pointing to my breast. My shoes were missing, bags gone, the silver slid from my ears, the tiny topaz I had been wearing slipped from my neck, watch unclasped, even my glasses had been coaxed from behind my ears.

In the hospital room I couldn't see. That was okay. A world blurry around the edges never bothered me.

I couldn't remember, and that was okay too. I knew I had been in an accident. I knew I had not gotten to the hospital by myself, that I could not have. I thought again how the kindness of people in this country outweighed their superstitions, like the belief that exposure to cold could cause anything from minor colds to a heart attack.

Even with my eyes closed, I felt the city, surrounded by water, sticky with salt.

I remembered Paul with his arm linked in mine and dragging me through the street. Don't wander off, he said to me at first, like he would to a child. He held my arm tight.

The minute I woke up in the hospital, I knew I wouldn't be able to stay in the city after they released me. I had been in and out of sleep for a day or so, if I understood the nurse. A consular official came and then left. There was the visa problem, and a crime.

Money was wired, and it hadn't been exchanged. I had forgotten the dull pine of American currency, the narrow bills smelling of clay. I tipped the boy who

208

brought the Western Union envelope twenty dollars because I didn't really want it. I didn't want to be stranded broke either, but I wasn't interested in being saved.

The day on Mount Erciyes, when Paul had grabbed our arms, Yasemin had asked him if he was trying to rescue us, and he had told her he only wanted something to hold on to.

There was less hurt than surprise at the sting of missing my friends. I asked the nurse about the periodic table postcard that had been in my pack.

"*Periyodik tablo var mı?*" I asked. *Is there a periodic table?*

"*Var,*" she said. *There is.* She looked puzzled, but pointed to the wall, where a Turkish table hung.

I carried the daypack for so long, had taken only a single thing of Yasemin's, and now it was lost.

Another day passed. My doctor was well spoken and explained I was in the Almanya Hastanesi, the German Hospital, in Istanbul's Taksim district, and he said that I had arrived by car, but the driver had declined to leave his name.

There are moments that take on an expansive quality, when you're looking at yourself through a wide-angle lens or under layers of glass.

Two police officers came for my statement, a male and a female. Both spoke quietly while the doctor translated. They wanted to know who had beaten me, and I said I had no memory of it. They could not have known how truthful I was being; that even the memories I did have seemed too distant to even belong to me. I was very clear to the police that I did not believe that the men I'd encountered were Turks, and I even tried to say it in Turkish, so that they would know that I would know a *Türk* when I saw one, but I fumbled so badly I'm not sure if they understood me.

It was the worst kind of accident—the foreign woman alone in a Muslim city.

Remembering what I could of it, with the weight of the hospital blankets and the prick of the drip line, I wondered if I saw something of the attacker's face, but I couldn't pull anything distinct out of the mash of the day's crowds.

A passport arrived. It was my name, but I didn't know the picture—my hair was long, dyed a red that was nearly crimson, permed. It had to be over a decade old. I placed this photograph as being from my mother's archives. There were the freckles fanned across my nose, but it was not my face anymore.

"They'll never let me on a plane with this," I told the boy who delivered it, the same boy who'd brought the money.

"We got a lot of message for you," he said. "Sometimes people are having problem and no one rings."

I wanted to take him in my arms, breathe his lemon cologne and the tang of coal smoke that permeated everyone's skin, get at the potatoey smell that came from washing in the tap water. To hold him and touch his black hair.

"You wouldn't believe," he said.

I wanted to ask him how they had identified me, but it wouldn't have been that hard. Probably I told the hospital my name, maybe my nationality.

It takes a phone call, only.

•

I was driven to the airport, escorted, I might say. The officers and the doctor from the German hospital helped me gently from one seat to a wheelchair, then to a new seat. I could walk but I didn't want to. I'd felt this kind of fatigue only once before: pregnant in summer, so slippery with my own sweat that even if I could have moved, I would not have gotten purchase. At the airport, I was dry, drained, and I felt that same deep tired. I suppose I could have fought, if I had wanted to.

And I would have to face my American life, eventually.

I fumbled with my new, heavy black glasses constantly. The fit was as off as the prescription. They had taken me to an optometrist at the hospital, but I'd barely paid attention as he flicked through the lenses on the phoropter.

The airplane was like any other. Every bump made me wonder when we would go down, so I prayed for a clean entry into the Atlantic, the splash sucked back under by our momentum, the way a perfect dive inverts the water. No more messes, I hoped, cabin doors hurling off and the unbuckled whooshed out immediately, the rest of us waiting for our seats to give.

I watched movies and tried not to think about Paul. I tried not to think about Yasemin. I wondered if I'd been wearing my wedding ring, if it would have still been on my finger, and I thought that probably it would not be. *So there*, I thought, *an explanation.*

At thirty-thousand feet there is no weather, only dark or day, and if I had a choice, I would have chosen dark.

•

We landed. Half a world from America and it takes only hours to return to the western United States. Flying west, time runs backward. It is noon in Milan, and then later, noon in New York. At each change, there was staff waiting for me to make sure I disembarked properly or, presumably, did not hobble through customs and back out into the world. Had I not been so tired, so deeply, deeply tired, I would have felt exotic, the fugitive caught and returning for judgment.

The airport staff was more concerned that I was comfortable and that I had been fed.

In Seattle, they were waiting: Julian, Anastasia, and my parents. A family. There was no luggage, only me and my purples. I liked these visible hurts—I liked looking like the garden after the cattle had been loosed upon it, like the scars on Paul's back.

I tried to think of myself as covered in birth-marks.

I thought, *I am new.*

I let the SeaTac staff assist me, and I kept my eyes closed. They had wheeled me through customs, who asked nothing, and I had put my passport back in my lap and turned my head to the side, and this was how they would have seen me come out of the gates.

I was not sure how I wanted them to feel—I was like an egg left too long uncollected, dirty shell, gone off inside, a center of wet feathers.

I did not stand to greet them, even though I could have. My cheap slippers, loaned from the hospital, were heavy on my feet. They leaned down, one by one, to embrace me, except for Anne who, at eight now, who had just had her birthday, was short enough just to come to the side of the chair. I pulled her to me—she looked so much older. I supposed so did I.

The rest of their voices were strange, the long *a* and hard *r* of an American accent.

My father, my mother. Alike with their old, translucent skin. Julian with a thick golden band at his finger—I had worn the match to it, a thin one with a tiny diamond stud, but now the place below my knuckle was covered in a splint, and below that, it was bare.

•

On the ground, I kept feeling for the earrings I'd been wearing, touching my empty lobes. They had been spiral, like a slinky stretched long. There had been a sharp bend where the metal hooked through the piercing—they fit tightly, and had been, consequently, one of the few pairs I had that were still mated, and I had been wearing them everywhere.

I rode in the far back of my parents' van, Julian and Anne in the middle seat.

I'd left the chair near the gates and let Julian help me through the parking garage. On my arm, his hand felt gloved. I was cold and shivered, and he pulled my body close to his for heat, and it was the same, like trying to touch through cloth.

I knew they were waiting for me to say something but I was as blank as I had ever been. I watched my father negotiate his way out of the airport and onto the interstate. It was Seattle, and so it rained.

I thought, *Thank you Allah for sending this water, let it wash me pure.* But the more I looked through the side window the more I knew this would not happen, that this was not divine rain, just the average Pacific stuff that would drizzle on until March, and it would bring gray in shades from sludge to silver, but I would not come clean.

My father drove us to our house on Jackson. Julian unlocked the door and they followed him inside. I went straight to the guestroom and lay down. I had painted this little room myself and it was sage, because sage seemed very neutral and homey, though I myself did not prefer green.

Julian knocked.

"I am very tired," I said, and I was.

"Laura," he said.

"I cannot have a homecoming just this minute," I said. I wanted to ask him if he'd gotten my message, if he'd known I'd been on my way back, if slowly.

"I need to talk to you alone. Can you understand that?"

"Yes," I said, and I did. "May I see my daughter?" I asked, and there was anger again, at requesting permission.

I heard Julian back away from the door and then Anastasia came in, her face framed by those gold curls, Julian's hair.

I was on my belly on the bed, my face turned toward the door.

"Close the door, sugar," I said, "then come sit with me."

She did. She was an obedient girl.

We didn't say anything, but she leaned into me and I put my arm around her.

I could not say I was happy to be there, on the musty guest mattress, but I was happy for the closeness of my daughter. There was something in me that didn't want to spare Anne anything, but I was at that moment, grateful, absolutely grateful I had not accidentally broken Julian's promise that I would return to her. She pulled her legs up and spooned into me, and we stayed there, quietly.

Perhaps fifteen minutes passed before my mother tapped the door and then came in. She stood over the side of the bed.

"You need to talk to your husband," she said.

"I will."

"You're home now. You'll be fine," she continued—the predictable, empty kind of comfort I didn't want. "You have us, you have Julian, you have Anne."

She was right.

215

Also, I had a hole in my heart, shaped like Paul, shaped mostly like Yasemin.

Shaped like a crescent, shaped like a star.

•

My bruises faded slowly. I am not a fast healer. I was glad; I wanted to keep them like India ink under my skin, as evidence.

"What *happened?*" Julian asked in a whisper that first night, after my parents had reluctantly left for a hotel. I was still in the guest bed.

I didn't know how to answer his question. I wanted to. I wanted to explain, first *A* then *B* and now *C*, but I didn't know how to say anything.

He put his hand on my head.

"Don't," I said, and he moved his palm away.

I wanted to know how they had found me so quickly, but I knew—a stranger is checked into a hospital, calls are made. I remembered registering at the embassy when I had thought I was only going on vacation. Address on file. Emergency contact information. Start to build a new life. Wake up woozy in a white-walled hospital.

Return plane.

"Julian," I said. "I was trying to get back."

"You made it," he said.

CHAPTER SIX

As a younger woman, before I met Julian, and even through our first few years, especially before our daughter, I enjoyed drinking to excess. Even if I still drank, I went through phases were I was less of a lush. To begin with, I loved the color of booze. Amber and smoke and burnt cherry. There were many mornings where I was left befuddled over what had happened the night before, and I would lie in my bed with my quilts cocooned around me and parse back through what I could remember.

This made for a long, slow waking up and gave the day a kind of dimness that I felt now. Though the pieces were all there, I was not sure of the pattern.

And even more than that, I was unsure of the point.

I was back in our pretty home. We had chosen all the tasteful colors. Mint, robin egg blue, fresh cream. It was the kind of place that always had enough clean linens and blankets and pillows for guests, always a decent bottle of wine in the pantry. There were many windows and sun, when there was some, streamed into every room. Jackson Street was close to the city center, in an older neighborhood. It was a home I had baked bread from scratch in, a home with a big stereo and a small television, and waxy refinished hardwood floors. We had worked very hard on it.

And after my forced return, I felt filth everywhere.

The Pull of It

The first summer after my job loss, when Anne was on break from school, I distracted myself with epic sessions of dress up and make-believe with her. That was the blessing of having a girl. When the holidays ended, I was still unemployed. It wasn't that Julian and I didn't keep things clean, it was more like I was discontent and looking for something in the cracks, in the rafters.

If I had done epic cleaning a year ago, now I took the house apart, and put it back together. Every closet, every drawer, every envelope filled with scraps of paper or rubber bands; I opened everything, sorted it, closed it up. I even pried the molding from around the bathroom floor—you wouldn't believe what's behind there, lint and pubic hair, and a few tiny spiders—and wiped it clean, tacked it back to the wall with invisible finishing nails.

I thought of my daughter. She was plowing through school, and I had missed her birthday in late July. I just wasn't aware of the days. Julian had told me, of course, but "next Wednesday" didn't mean much to me then.

I loved her, she was what brought me back, she held me.

I remember the night I got pregnant. I had known it would happen. Julian and I had been married for a few years, and we'd been recently discussing children. I was drunk again and on our walk home from the local pub, I saw, through a street-level window, the last moments of a thirty-something party. I had just turned twenty-eight. Parents had scooped up their toddlers from where they'd been napping on the couches or back bedrooms, and at least half the people had a sleepy child in their arms. I knew these people would buckle up, that no one would drive home too loaded, that if they had nasty things to say to each other they'd save it for another day. The children had turned these ordinary people decent, and after our parties and my dreams of long ago loves, I wanted it.

And I told Julian.

And it took one time.

I had been off of my birth control for months. Even that early on in our marriage, the turn had happened, and we were rarely having sex, and even if we did, neither of us could come, so Julian, at some point, would give up and plod into the bathroom and finish himself off, and I would wait in the dark bed and wonder what was going on with us, and in the morning before work, after he was gone, I would masturbate while I thought of nothing.

So when I told Julian what I had seen at the party, he came at me with a passion I hadn't seen in him since our wedding night. With a passion I thought we both had given up.

And I didn't know how to tell him it had all been a mistake. Not a mistake. A misunderstanding.

And here was Anne; our daughter, quieter than her father or me, spilling vials of glitter onto glue and drawing on scraps, decorating her room with cutouts of pretty paper she salvaged from the trash. She had an eye for it, angling her homemade stencils to pull a star or flower or half of a letter from a package of almond soap or sack from the gourmet markets where Julian shopped.

It was the effort he made for me, shopping. We had always had fresh vegetables and interesting fruits: quince and pomegranate, Asian pears.

What I can say for Julian: he gave me anything I wanted.

That's the way marriage goes sometimes, I suppose. As our friends around us paired and coupled off, I would say, *Congratulations.* I would say, *I hope this is exactly what you want.* But you can't know, ever, until the marriage is happening, and by then, you've already battened down every available hatch. The blood has been drawn, the results filed. You've been witnessed to have pledged yourself.

I liked Julian. He was great sometimes. Even after Anne was born, we did still talk, about Anne, or politics, or the finer points of sedimentology. We talked about public policy. We talked about any number of things that some ordinary lives never touch on.

We didn't talk about why, after a few tousles around the time Anne was conceived, we'd mostly stopped having sex again. We didn't talk about why we were talking about the natural and social sciences instead of the way we spiraled inward. We didn't talk about the way that if we didn't read the paper or get a nice dose of CNN we'd have nothing, really, to discuss.

It was easy, though, to avoid any real topics. Relationships, I had come to think, were like that: like the edible parts of a snail. Sort of squishy in the same way a full bag of kitchen garbage is—soft and sweetly, slowly spoiling. But perfect it—rip out the innards, purge the guts, and pour it all back into the shell—and it's coveted gourmet. It's stylish and satisfying. It's butter and magic.

Julian and I, though, we liked our hiding places just as much as any in the molluscan class, so I can't blame him for the fact we would talk heliciculture before we'd talk about our insides.

I can't say I had no idea how badly, even if I clung to the house, I had wanted to be away from him and what I had come to think of as The Marriage. Sometimes, after the return, I would look at him and think, *Christ, why are you here?* His shoulders, when he'd be at the kitchen counter, doing something normal, like grinding coffee, seemed so ridiculously enormous, like two wheel wells.

When I'd first met him, I'd loved his big hands and broad fingers. He cupped my face in a very particular way—tips of his fingers behind my ears and his palm on my chin, supporting my head like one might with an infant.

Maybe it was time moving that made his touch less endearing.

We were in our third stage of separation by now, and I was still sleeping on the guest bed.

The second time we stopped being intimate nearly altogether, I went through a period where if we were in our bed and he reached to touch me, I would say, "Julian, did you wash your hands?"

Sometimes, he would roll over, toss back the covers, and slip into the bathroom. I'd hear the water on and the splashing while he soaped up. He would come back to me with his nails neat and his skin smooth, touched with the smell of my almond soap. And sometimes he would pull back from me, turn, and go to sleep.

The thing was, I didn't care how it turned out either way, as long as I didn't have his dirty paw between my legs.

•

I wished Anne was with me, but it was September, and she was back in school again. I had missed her birthday while I was in the hospital, on the twenty-seventh of July, when I was in and out of the fog, and then I'd missed the start of her school year by not paying attention to how quickly the calendar was moving. I would have felt sorry if I could have found a way to fit it into everything else.

I would spend my days doing things like picking out an iron on the Internet, printing out the product information for Julian, leaving it on the kitchen table.

And he would spend his evenings doing things like coming home with a box, a perfect rectangle, with the shining triangle inside.

This marked the start of a new phase. My phase of steel.

Complementing this was the splint on my ring finger. I pretended it was broken, and I refused to see an American physician. That would mean leaving the house. Julian brought home a newer brace for it, one a little less used, and I wore it. I was still wearing it, weeks later. I took it off every day, washed, and put it back on.

Part of it was that I liked to click it against metal
stair railings, against glass. I waited for Julian to tell me
to stop. Nervous sounds, like drumming fingers, drove
him mad. He said nothing. I tapped out the beat of any
song I could think of. To him it must have been the
same series of *clink clink clink* on the ceramic
countertops, but I heard saz, I heard drums.

Part of it was that I didn't want him to see that
the wedding band was missing, because though it most
likely would have been taken, I wasn't wearing it, so I
couldn't know. He hadn't asked and I hadn't offered.

I told Julian he didn't need to send his shirts out
anymore, now that I had this miraculous iron.

"Miraculous?" he said to me from where he
stood in the kitchen.

"It's engineering," I said. I thought I sounded
delightfully coy, and I shook the ice in my cocktail.

And I was right. I tapped my brace against the
slick of the iron, and Julian's shirts were as crisp as
origami paper, our cotton sheets as smooth as Anne's
skin. I had never had an iron like this, puffing steam as
thick as cigar smoke. Yasemin would have been proud.

I also continued to do the usual things—wash
the sugar bowl and defrost the freezer. I hosed off the
upper and the lower deck.

I thought of Yasemin while I cleaned.

Since it was fall by then, the yard needed
tending. Nothing had been done with it all summer.
Back when I first lost my job, I had at first been
ambitious but then managed to miss the earliest
annuals; now I wondered if my irises would bloom ever

again, but I didn't cross onto the lawn. Really, past the deck, I didn't go outside.

I held my iron like a weapon.

I ordered Middle Eastern cookbooks and supplies: cardamom and special ground red peppers; a string of cleaned, dried sheep intestines; pressure pots and Syrian tea. I was keeping myself busy.

I felt like I was grieving, and I thought maybe I could just move through the stages of grief. I knew them from a few years of therapy in my twenties, before I met Julian. I thought, *denial, anger, bargaining, depression, acceptance*, why not?

The cookbooks were helpful. I prepared vast pots of rice and garbanzo beans, warm garlicky yogurt and any kind of lamb. Peppers drowned in oil and tomato. I served Julian olives and goat cheese for breakfast, made him strong tea. I made the cups sing with my metal brace, and he said nothing.

The cooking helped me remember now, instead of forget.

On weekdays, at three in the afternoon, Anne arrived home from school and I started dinner.

I, still, after all the years she'd been with us, could not see my face in hers. I had tried. I had studied myself in the mirror, my straight, light brown hair, my wide, freckled nose. Her legs, her arms, the way she bent her elbows, she seemed to belong entirely to herself.

I liked it when Anne was home; I had missed her in a way I was only beginning to understand.

She was still a quiet child. Contained. Average sized for her age, not particularly pretty, but there was sharpness in her hazel eyes. The color she had gotten from her father, but that look, I thought, that look—like, *You don't have to tell me twice, or I am not amenable to these constant interruptions,* or *Can you see the way the light made this shadow?*—certainly came from me.

Thoughtfully, once she stepped off the bus, walked the block and a half from her stop, she would pause on our porch and pull off the notes Julian's friends had left during the day. If there was a package I had not retrieved, and it was not too heavy, she would drag it in the door.

She would say, without fail, "Mom! I brought in the deliveryables."

I didn't know where she had heard this word or how it had gotten twisted for her. I didn't know where she had learned these types of tiny kindnesses. I didn't know who taught her to lock the door when she came inside, or who had shown her how to trip the latch on the hidden key holder (a planter filled with a failing climbing rose) in case she found the door secured when she came home.

If the telephone rang in those hours before Julian came back from his office downtown, Anne answered it. So politely.

"Clarey residence," she would say, like a professional would. Like a visitor might. Mostly, it was one of my parents. Anne would say, "I'm sorry, my mom can't come to the phone right now."

My mother on the other line, something like: Anne, honey, what's she doing right now?

Then my daughter's voice, lower, the loud, airy whisper kids figure only the person they're talking to can hear, "Grandma, I don't know!"

•

Julian sent an old friend of ours around, Janine. I was glad when I looked through the peephole in the front door; I expected my mother on the porch, in from out of town again, but there was Janine, looking back at me through the convex glass, her lips pressed in and her eyes opened up a little expectantly.

I made her clear tea in my immaculate cups, and we sat on the second-floor balcony off the master bedroom and shared cigarettes.

"He's worried, you know," she told me.

I had known Janine for years, for all of my adult life and a fair portion of my childhood. She had four children, three with her husband and a foster child named Blake, ten years old and scars across his back; he was the same age as us when we'd become friends. He'd lived with them for nearly two years and still wouldn't talk about the scars. He'd stopped stealing money, stopped hoarding food, stopped wetting the bed, but wouldn't talk. They sent him to a child psychologist, who gave him Legos to play with and smelly markers with which to draw. The psychologist sent some of the drawings home with him, and brought Janine in to see what he'd built with the Legos: always houses with no windows and no doors.

I liked him, his deep green eyes and angry smile. I wished she'd brought him, but she'd come alone.

After a pause, she said, "Julian is worried you might try to hurt yourself."

I looked at her.

Always people think this is the worst thing—that someone might try to die, but it's not. If you want to die maybe you still care a little bit. Maybe you think they'll all be sorry, or maybe you think of release. What it means is something still hurts, something can hurt. If you are past the point of dying, well, that's where the worry really is.

"I've been doing really well," I said. "Did you see the house when we came through? It's gorgeous."

I was proud of what Yasemin had taught me.

Was I preparing?

"You're obsessing over it," she said. "He says you do nothing but clean and cook all day long. He says you virtually ignore Anne."

"I do not ignore her. We spend time in the afternoon. She helps me. And I do my best with her," I said. That was true. I looked at Janine, her slim hips and little high breasts, thick hair, brown bag hair. "I'm doing my best with everything."

"Well, that's what you can do, I guess."

"Thanks," I said.

"Your house *is* gorgeous. But your yard looks horrible," she said, teasing.

"I know." I'd lost hope for anything intentional to grow, the garden was so choked with weeds. Once I had staked tomatoes and grown basil.

"I don't want to ask you anything you don't want to talk about," she said. "But we all wonder."

I thought of something I'd heard from a radio psychologist once—*Everything before the word but is bullshit*—and pulled on the long white cigarette.

"Laura?" Janine asked.

I looked at her again. My cigarette had burned all the way down.

"You've got to come back, okay?" she said.

"I'm right here," I said.

"I know you are. But you're somewhere else too."

I nodded.

"I miss you. I haven't seen you in ages."

"I miss you too," I said, but I didn't know if I meant it. "I should start dinner."

"Julian said you've become a good cook. Maybe we can swap recipes," she said, her pretty mouth turned up in a small smile. She wasn't silly enough to really suggest that we get out our index cards and trade. She was only trying—just like I was.

I stood up, held my arm over the railing of the balcony, and tossed the last of my cup of tea onto the ragged grass.

•

I think Julian thought that what I had was just an average case of middle-class blues, but it had to be more. Like I said, I'd been through therapy before, and once I hit on this idea of grieving, of loss, I felt almost like I had a plan.

The day after Janine visited, before Anne was home from school and Julian from work, I went into the office. I used to spend a lot of time in that room, but now it was Julian's place. He paid the bills and filed the receipts, he skulked around on the computer, probably still always working late. I sometimes went online to order things, but I had ignored the business end of The Marriage for enough time that it had almost ceased to be real.

I lived in our home, but my heart was with Yasemin and Paul, out in the unknown, beating against nothing.

I found some index cards, and I wrote out each part:

I deny that my finger is not injured.

I am angry that the threshold beyond the house is uncrossable.

I will bargain for the immunity of my daughter toward the situations of adults.

I am depressed about the garden.

I accept that my husband does not understand my predicaments.

I flipped through the five cards. They made about as much sense as anything else. I thought of calling Anne's school and telling them there was an emergency at home, but I was pretty sure that they wouldn't deliver her, and I would have to go pick her up, thus creating an actual emergency, the emergency of me behind the wheel. Not, it seemed, a good idea.

My next idea was to make a cocktail. Since this was something I could actually act on, I gathered up the index cards and went to the kitchen. I loved how the ice was so clear and how it snapped on the first pour of alcohol. I loved the glint of the clean glass against the smear of my fingerprints.

I read my cards again. I sipped my whiskey. It was too early to begin dinner, but too late to start any real project for the day. I wasn't really sure what I'd done with the morning, besides my five sentences.

I tried to think about how Julian might see me, or what he might do if he were me—he was always a good problem solver, but I think I didn't want to be solved. Without Paul and Yasemin, I only wanted my drink, my Anne, my memories, and the house.

For now, the house would keep me safe.

•

In my second absence, Julian had taken even more to our girl than the first time I had left him. He would have had to. He would have had to step up to his *responsibility*. I stopped being angry with him for taking her to my parents' house when I saw how much closer they too had gotten to her.

There was also the feeling that nothing had changed, even after I *came back*. I shouldn't say I came back. I should say that, again, I unpacked my suitcase. In the evenings, we still sat silently across from each other at the table, and we listened to our daughter singsong about her day.

So I was surprised when Julian said, at dinner one evening, "Anne's got parent-teacher conferences at school, so I'll need you to be dressed and ready around eleven on Thursday. She's home all day; your mom is going to come by and watch her."

My mother. I think things were not good between my father and her either. They'd had their problems—who didn't?—and in the years that I and my brothers had been gone, things had only gotten worse. She was staying off and on in Seattle with a friend of hers, Marilee, who she had worked with once, and who was now divorced and trying to work her body and her brain around having multiple sclerosis. It was a common disease in Washington, strangely so. My mother wondered if it was caused by spending so much time in the eastern agricultural part of the state, where brightly colored bi-planes blanketed the apple valleys with velvety loops of pesticide.

I did not think the eleven o'clock time frame was acceptable. Around eleven, I would be wanting a cocktail. Around ten-thirty, Julian and my mother would show up, likely in tandem, likely in some coordinated effort that involved her setting Marilee's oven timer and Julian syncing his Blackberry. Would they work together to block the exits? I would be wanting to contemplate my cocktail. Maybe my mother would even bring Marilee, on a crutch, for effect. At ten-fifteen, I would have already prepared for the contemplation by have a conversation with myself regarding whether the ice was fresh and whether there was an agreeable mixer. The cocktail, it should be said, would happen regardless.

"It's too soon for me," I said.

Had I left the house on my own since returning?

Once. A coffee emergency. For his part, I can say Julian brought home everything I asked for. "Or maybe I shouldn't go. Maybe she doesn't want me there," I suggested.

"Anne won't be there," Julian said. Many things he said to me were statements, and anyway, I had known that she wouldn't be there. "You should talk to her teacher."

"I met her in the fall," I said. Many things that I had been saying to him lately were statements as well.

"Do you know what it was like for me to go on my own last time?" he asked.

I did. Of course I did. "I've been to the school by myself for these things before," I told him.

"It's different," he said, "I was working."

There it was.

I thought about what to say—it was true that I'd left him alone in a very, very different way. But I also felt like now I was working extremely hard, at contemplating, at indexing.

I would have memories in flashes of Paul's art show, the weird looping tape and the meat stinking up the room.

I resolved then to memorize the periodic table so that I could not lose it again.

He stared at me, and he looked just like our daughter, face framed with curls, with disbelief.

And then I felt something turn in me, like suddenly I had some of my strength back, and I thought, *Okay, yes, I will grant you this favor.*

But it wasn't like that at all.

Outside of the house, I was scared.

I dreaded Thursday all week, as I had plenty of time for it. Three long, slow days. Three days of fresh ice.

When my mother arrived, I was dressed and ready to go as Julian had told me to be. My contemplation had told me it would be easier to just play along. The day was already different with Anne home instead of in school.

My finger was still set in the brace, and as Julian drove, I tapped it on the dash of the car, but the sound was nothing. *Thunk. Thunk.* I kept tapping out the beat of any song I could think of. To him it must have been the same serious of *clink clink clink* on the ceramic countertops, but I still heard the call to prayer, I heard the *zing* of the Ankara metro.

I went for the window and Julian stopped me with a look.

"You've got to get that looked at. Probably it can come off."

"I like it," I said.

"Your finger might be rotting away in there and you'd never know," he said.

"Yes I would," I said.

"How?"

"I would smell it."

He didn't have to worry. I took the brace off once a day and flexed my finger and cleaned the skin. I knew it wasn't even really broken, at the most extreme end of the scale, mildly fractured, and probably not even that. If I had really broken it, I might have gotten a cast.

Plaster. No music there.

The Pull of It

In some other time, before we soured and I went off, we would have walked to Anne's school, and we would have taken sneaky looks into the houses along the way, commenting on the cheesy Monet prints or the odd spoon collection on the living room walls. I would have occasionally broken off a cutting from someone's street-side flower bed and dropped the stalk guiltily into my purse, and I would have dutifully tried to start it, with the intention of planting, as soon as we got home. (Every one of these died.)

Mostly we would hold hands and congratulate ourselves for being us, not them. Now that I thought of it, I remembered it was only me clumping along and making noisy comments about people I'd never meet.

I suppose he was kind, my Julian.

"You know what else? I'm afraid," I said to him.

"Then go ahead," he said, and he meant it.

I moved my pinky to my window and started with the beginning of Leonard Cohen.

I tried to leave you. Tap. Tap. *I don't deny.*

I closed the book on us, at least a hundred times.

"I like that one," Julian said.

Was he lying?

I'd wake up every morning by your side.

•

I froze at the school. Cohen's molasses voice turned to sludge.

"I can't go in," I said.

He took me by the arm. I realized how well I knew his touch.

234

The tiny desks and tiny chairs. Drawings made with tiny hands. I could have picked out Anne's on the bulletin board, even if I hadn't seen her name spelled out in wobbly letters. All of it: *Anastasia.* I hadn't known she preferred it.

"I asked them to draw a picture of their family," Miss Corey said.

She looked exactly like I remembered and like I hoped she wouldn't, young and pretty and fresh with new ideas, flushed with the joy of loving her job. Brown shoulder-length hair pulled back sensibly into clips, flower print A-line dress snug at the bust.

She said Anastasia was quiet, code for sullen. Creative, she said, code for weird. Bright, she said, code for potentially anti-social. I knew. I had been called those things before.

I focused on the bulletin board, the yellow suns and green grasses, the matchstick people holding hands. My daughter's was different than some of the others. Julian was represented by a necktie and that delightfully curly Anne had drawn me wearing the pair of spiral earrings that I'd worn constantly before they'd been stolen, before I was the kind of person who could leave people without actually doing them the courtesy of leaving.

I was almost sorry then I couldn't give them the reunion they must have wanted. My Anne, my Julian.

•

That next morning I woke up and I went to our porch. I thought, *This is what it's like to be stuck.* I

235

thought, *This is exactly what I was trying to avoid.* Which might even have been true.

•

Janine came by more frequently. One thing I loved about her was how she always came in a cloud of noise. She walked loudly, she wore swishy clothing; she'd spent so much time around her children that she'd forgotten what an inside voice sounded like.

Janine could never sneak up on anyone. Plus, she wasn't the type.

At first, when I starting locking the door to her, she let herself in with the spare key that I'd forgotten she had. I thought about changing the locks, but that seemed like so much work.

She came by the next week after the conferences, and she plopped down on the sofa.

"Make me one of those," she shouted from the living room.

"What?" I said. I was in the kitchen, mixing vodka.

"Don't hide that you're drinking, because you can't hide anything from me. I have four children. I have eyes in the back of my head and the front of my head and probably on my ass, too."

"Okay," I said. "It's vodka cran."

"I like mine with lime," she said.

I brought her the cocktail. The cushions on the couch were smooth and neat. I'd vacuumed them that morning, drawing the hose attachment across the upholstery in long, smooth strokes, and I remembered Yasemin's disdain for the vacuum.

"Cheers," I said, and clinked my glass to hers. The ice tinkled.

"How do you say 'cheers' in Turkish?" she asked.

"Şerefe," I said. The word felt rich on my tongue.

"Share..." she said.

"Yes," I said. "*Share-if-a*, like the letter a." I liked the sound of this word.

"What's *vodka*?" she asked.

"Vodka," I said.

"What's *cranberry*?"

"I don't know. But 'berry' I think is something like *dut*."

"Okay, I'll have another one," she said. Janine looked at me like she did sometimes, a little mischievous and with an almost false naïveté, like once when she had asked me about how I shaved my bikini line and I gave her a detailed description, labia and all, she laughed and said, "I think I'll wax."

Her eyes were very brown. I had always thought she was pretty in an understated way. I admired her manner with her children, and I admired her handiness. We both had that country-person competency. When Janine's children were small they were forever bending her glasses, and she had this practiced, fearless way of bending them back into shape. "If they break, they break," she would say. "I already can't wear them." As far as I knew, she never got a proper adjustment unless her prescription changed and she needed a new pair.

"You don't love him anymore, do you?" she said.

I nearly dropped my glass—it tipped from my hand but I recovered and only spilled a little on the leg of my pants. The sofa was dry.

"Janine," I said.

"I know," she said. "I know it's not a yes or no question. But your face looks like a *no*."

My ice seemed to be melting quickly; the tinkling had stopped. "You're right," I said.

"What now?" she asked.

"I don't know," I said.

We sat there on the sofa for a while. Condensation sweated off my cocktail and dripped onto my pants in the same place I'd spilled. Janine and I had known each other for years—we'd been girls together, and confided everything. She talked me through everything from leaving boyfriends to pregnancy ankles.

It was impossible to me that we'd have nothing to say.

•

Even though she was not particularly fast to forgive me, Anastasia did. As the weeks passed, she became slowly less standoffish, and she started to let me do things that she wouldn't at first, like coming into her room to comfort her if she had a nightmare. She let me brush her hair in long, smooth strokes, until it shined. She let me help her with her homework.

In her room I saw some of the postcards I had sent her, taped to her wall, and when I asked Julian about the rest of them, he said the school counselor had told him to be very careful with my messages, and when I took them down one day to see what I had written, the ones that had gotten through were all cheerful, *Mommy is on vacation* notes.

In the afternoons after school, Anne and I made flashcards together, and I went through basic spelling words and multiplication tables with her. I held up 6x12 to her and she said *72* and she held up *Fe* and I said *Iron*; she held up K and I said *Potassium*; she held up *Au* and I said *Gold*, and I rubbed the spot on my left hand where the band was missing and I'd finally removed the splint.

Julian tolerated me. I had sex with him once or twice. What else could I do? I thought it was worth a try.

I dreamt of Paul and Yasemin, and then mostly only of Yasemin, and I woke to my actual life.

My mother ended her last, long visit and went back home, to my father—she knew that not everything was okay, but I think she was where I was. You do what you can and you go on. We talked almost every day and the five-hour drive that separated us felt no greater or shorter than a ten-hour time difference had.

I realized one day that Anne could tell me if I had answered correctly with the periodic table flashcards without even looking.

"Maybe you'll like chemistry," I said to her.

"It's more fun than spelling," she said.

"What's *Pt?*" I asked her.

"Platinum," she quickly said. "It's a metal."

"It's a very shiny metal," I said.

"Like silver?" she asked.

"Yes, like silver, but brighter." I said. "Thank you for helping," I said to her. "It's very important to me to learn this."

She didn't say anything, but she reached for the flashcards. She flipped through and held up *Md.*

"Mendelevium," I said.

"You always get that one," she said, and went digging through the stack for something harder.

CHAPTER SEVEN

When the bus paused for lunch at Blue City, I checked the progress of the nearby poplar farms, and I imagined living in the green-shuttered house with the empty aqua pool on the edge of the roadside pear orchard. I had been in this place before, a nowhere bus stop on the road north from Ankara where we would take the twenty-minute break customary for every three hours of between-city bus travel.

I shook Anne awake, gently. It had been a very long journey, and she had been very good.

•

Julian had sat me down at the kitchen table. The days had gotten gray again, and Anne and I had decorated the house for Halloween, lopsided jack-o-lanterns sagging on the porch steps and one perched atop a scarecrow we'd made of Julian's old clothes stuffed with leaves. We'd tried to keep the leaf-man up with a broom handle, but he kept falling, slumped against the siding. He looked drunk and tired, his smile jagged. Anne loved it.

"I have a partnership opportunity in Vancouver," Julian said. "It would be very good for the business."

"Vancouver, Washington, or Vancouver, BC?" I asked.

"BC," he said.

"That's not so far from here," I said. And it wasn't—a quick trip on the seaplanes out of Seattle's Lake Union or a couple hours drive.

"I wasn't planning that you'd come," he said.

I hadn't been thinking he was going to move there. I thought he'd commute. I thought Anne and I would have a lot of time at home together.

"Okay," I said. I had a lot of questions, but I didn't ask any of them. He was probably counting on that I would understand, and I did understand.

I reached my hand across the table to Julian, and he took it. His fingers were warm, and I felt our old closeness.

It took a little time. We didn't file any serious paperwork, and we were careful about how we talked about it with friends. Anne was staying with me, because I was still not working and Julian would be very busy with his new venture. He didn't want her to change schools, and I agreed with him. I wasn't sure it was a good idea for her to have another parent be gone, and I told him this. I thought he might argue, but he didn't.

"I know," he said. We both looked at the floor.

We went through the process of passporting Anne so she could visit. When I showed my own passport, I blushed at the picture and the memory. Two months had passed, and I thought of Yasemin every day.

By Thanksgiving, he was all but gone, his office entirely packed, and just his carry-on suitcase left.

My parents came for dinner and my friend Janine and her children. I made a traditional dinner, no

Turkish sides thrown in, no dishes of peppers and yogurt on the table.

I'd stopped drinking, knowing it would be just me and Anne, and when Julian had asked me that morning if I would be okay alone, I thought about it hard. My bruises were all gone now, my finger healed. The assault, of everything, was not what haunted me, it was almost the opposite—now that something like it had happened to me, maybe it didn't have to happen again, or to Anne.

After dinner we had pie and chatted in the living room, while the kids watched a movie and my father napped.

My mother had been pleased when I told her she was welcome to the guest room, rather than staying with her friend Marilee, pleased that Julian and I were sleeping together again.

In the morning, he was leaving early for Canada, and before we went to wake Anne and get her into the car, Julian had made me promise that I wouldn't do anything stupid.

Define "stupid," I had thought.

•

It had been a challenge to get permission for a visa when I'd willfully let my tourist credentials expire, but I was good at paperwork, and I had time. I paid a fine out of my own bank account I'd set up, and I got a new passport photo.

In the first weeks, Julian was back almost every weekend, to see Anne, but already I saw how they were separating, and already I saw how he would have to earn her back if he ever came home. *It wouldn't be impossible,* I wanted to tell him.

We had Christmas together. When the new year came, I had the night I had wanted at the party we'd gone to the year before—just me and Anne at home alone. I thought it was only Yasemin who could have made it better.

When Julian emailed me in early January, he said he wouldn't be able to make it back for at least three weeks, maybe a month.

I had a window.

I hired movers to put everything in two separate storage units. I found renters, who were ready immediately. Luck everywhere.

I carried the key to one of the storage units with me now; mine and Anne's. The key to the other I left with the renters. I had told them it was a complicated situation and they had seemed sympathetic, and this explanation seemed to clarify why the rent was so low.

"If a man who says he is my husband or the owner of this property comes around," I said, "Please give him this envelope." This raised an eyebrow, but they agreed.

Inside, of course, the key. And also, a copy of the one-year rental contract, and a folded piece of lined notebook paper.

I am sorry for everything. Anne is with me. You are not living in the house, so I didn't think you would mind. We put so much work into it, it seems it shouldn't sit empty. They pay me, into my account directly. If you want half, send me an email. Let's talk about legal custody. Thank you for our daughter. Janine has details.

Janine was the only person I had told.

"Do you think he could do anything to you?" she asked. "I'm not sure this is a great idea. It seems sort of illegal."

"I disappeared," I said, "but he has moved, away from us. Permanently. He said he's getting residency."

"You might look crazier to a court," she said.

"Maybe," I said. "Maybe not."

"Just go," she said. "But stay in touch. I'll visit you."

And then the day before we were set to leave, I balked. I looked around the empty house. I looked at Anastasia and how hard I had missed her. I said her name, and it echoed against the bare walls and the clean floors.

"What?" she said.

"Nothing," I said. We had just two inflatable mattresses and our bags. The mattresses and the bedding would go into the garage in the morning.

I had the phone scheduled to be disconnected, but when I picked up the receiver in the kitchen, there was still a dial tone, so I punched Julian's number. It was like those desperate mornings and nights, trudging back and forth from Yasemin's, but without the credit card swipe. The phone was one of the mounted kind, and the cord was very long, so I stretched it out and clicked shut the door to the pantry.

When Julian answered, he sounded worried. It was late, and I rarely called.

"I'm going back," I told him, and the silence was so deep I thought we'd been disconnected, and then finally I heard him on the other side, not so far away, just across the border, and he coughed and cleared his throat and asked me why.

It was hard to tell him, but I tried. We talked for a long time, in a way we hadn't talked in years. A few times I came out to check on Anne, but she was fine, reading on her mattress.

I told him everything, from how I had never planned to stay gone for so long the first time, to how I had been planning to leave again without letting him know. I told him I was angry about our last years together, and I missed how we were in our first. I told him he had been mostly good to me, better than most would be, and that I was grateful for his patience.

He didn't say much, except that he thought this might happen.

"I would like to say goodbye to Anastasia," he said. "And to you."

"So do it," I said, like I had said all those years ago when he said he wanted to spend the rest of his life with me.

And he did. He hung up and drove through the night, and when he stepped into our empty house, he opened his arms, and I stayed there with him, like our old times, until the light came through the sky.

I wondered if he was letting Anne go too easily, but he'd gotten a year with her alone, and we made a deal then. If it were too much change for her, I would come back. If he missed us, he should come to us. If I needed to move on to somewhere, I would tell him.

It felt good to be on his side again.

•

I bought food at the cafeteria, soup and bread. I nodded at the people from my bus, nodded at the people traveling from other destinations or with other lines. I held a tray in one hand, Anne's hand in the other. We sat near a window and ate. The nose of the bus had been pointed toward the mountains all morning, and I could pick out Mount Erciyes in the distance.

I took Anne to the toilet. I washed my face.

Onur said he would meet us here, and I'd been looking for his rattly car with the smashed in trunk.

He'd been surprised when I had phoned him, but not as surprised as I had thought he would be. I would return, I told him, maybe I could help at the shop. We would find a tutor for Anne. It would be an unparalleled event for the village gossips. He said he took flowers to Yasemin's grave. He wanted to know if I could tell him which were her favorites, and I didn't know, but later I called him back and told him to bring geraniums, after germanium, *Gr*, a metal in the carbon group on the periodic table.

If he didn't show, I wasn't sure what I would do—continue on to Kayseri, maybe. I didn't know anyone besides Paul's wife, and for all I knew, Paul was back with her, making a winter soup and sculpting. I hoped he was, though I wasn't sure I was ready to see him. Or I could have waited a few hours and taken the bus back to Ankara.

Another exit, this time a little better planned. I wished Anne was older—we had talked about what was happening, but I wasn't sure she could understand it. When she had woken up in the morning before we left, she was surprised to see Julian there. He'd slept on the floor between us. They had talked in the yard for some time, and then he carried her outside to meet our taxi.

I patted my face dry. I didn't look too bad, considering how far we had traveled. Anne came out from the stall and I took her hand again.

We walked into the bright winter day.

I saw him there, then.

The dark brown hair, with a little more gray than I remembered at the temples. He was leaning against a modest but new car, smoking in the sunlight.

I gripped Anne's hand a little tighter and went toward him.

"*Merhaba*," I said as we approached. *Hello.*

"*Hoş Geldin*," he said. *Welcome*, in the informal tense.

The last time I had seen Onur, we had kissed on the cheeks while saying goodbye at his home. We kissed this way again, in greeting.

Then he kneeled, to shake Anne's hand. She smiled at him and shook back.

I had thought deeply about what Onur and I had in common—nothing really, except that we had loved the same woman and still grieved for her.

"We should go?" he said.

"Yes," I said, and I pointed to our luggage that was piled near the bus.

I looked at him. I wondered what Yasemin would think. I hoped she would understand how her country felt like the beginning of home to me. I hoped she would understand that what bound Onur and me together was her, even though we didn't know each other well enough to have a real friendship. Yasemin had never wanted an arranged marriage, but she had arranged something like it with us now.

When I'd tried to exit America the first time, I'd done it wrong—it wasn't the United States as a country I was trying to leave, and it wasn't right without my daughter. My parents would be angry again, my brothers confused, but it was clear, like when Yasemin and I washed and cleaned and scraped, making each room in the boardinghouse new, every day, that it was possible to start over. It felt right to have made even a small peace with Julian. We'd agreed to work out something sensible with visitation.

And if we stayed, I didn't know how life would look with Onur, but I knew we could raise Anne. I hoped she would keep with chemistry, and that we would have a simple life among the wool and rock of Anatolia, thinking of Yasemin every day, and living in her stead.

ABOUT THE AUTHOR

WENDY J. FOX was raised in rural Washington state, and lived in Turkey in the early 2000s. She holds an MFA from The Inland Northwest Center for Writers and is a frequent contributor to literary magazines and blogs. Her debut collection *The Seven Stages of Anger and Other Stories* won Press 53's 2014 competition for short fiction. She currently resides in Denver, where she is at work on a second novel.

Cover art by Nathan Brutzman
www.nthnart.com